I0598664

A SOFT PLACE TO FALL

LIZ FLAHERTY

A Soft Place to Fall
Copyright © 2022 Liz Flaherty
Published by Singing Tree Publishing
Cover Art by NFaRH Author Services

All rights reserved. No part of this book may be used or reproduced in any manner whatsoever without written permission of the author. Contact Information: lizkflaherty@gmail.com

This is a work of fiction. Names, characters, places, and incidents either are the product of the author's imagination or are used fictitiously, and any resemblance to actual persons living or dead, business establishments, events, or locales, is entirely coincidental.

eBook editions are licensed for your personal enjoyment only. eBooks may not be re-sold, copied or given away to other people. If you would like to share an eBook edition, please purchase an additional copy for each person you share it with.

Published in the United States of America
Second Singing Tree Edition, 2023
Electronic Edition ISBN: 978-0-9971637-7-3
Paperback Edition ISBN: 978-0-9971637-8-0
Publishing History
First Harbourlight Edition, 2013
Electronic Edition ISBN 978-1-61116-251-6
Paperback Edition ISBN 978-1-61116-271-4

For Duane, who's been my soft place to fall since that lovely day in May in 1971. You're still my hero.

CHAPTER 1

SPRINGTIME

Freedom.

Earline McGrath didn't know whether to laugh or cry, so she went into the garden and planted carrots. Nash hated carrots.

This morning they'd met oh-so-civilly in his brother's law office to finalize the division of thirty years' accumulation of things like DVD players and Christmas tree ornaments with "Logan, Fist Graid" written on them in glitter glue. Now it seemed important to her to do something her husband disliked. Planting carrots made more sense than rearranging furniture and was easier on the back even if it was hard on the knees.

Somewhere in the nightmare that was the three-car garage built to look like a wing on their pseudo-Victorian house, there were some kneepads from when the girls played high school volleyball. Early needed to find them. Only thing was, she'd find other stuff, too. Baby sleepers with spit-up stains, old diaries she should have burned years ago, and early marriage melamine dishes that would make her eyes sting and turn her heart into skip-a-beat mush.

They'd married the day after Nash graduated, when Early was

barely sixteen, just finishing up her sophomore year at the tiny high school in the middle of nowhere, Kentucky. She'd been eight weeks pregnant, but hardly anyone had known except Early's friends Mary Brad, Lou Ann, and Emily. Even when she gave birth to Evan seven months later and he weighed in at nearly nine pounds, she'd scarcely looked pregnant.

But, regardless of how she looked, her water broke in the produce department of Waylon's Supersaver, where Nash was peeling outer leaves off heads of cabbage for minimum wage. Patty Waylon had taken one look at the mess in aisle three and hollered, "Nash McGrath, put down those cabbages and get her to the hospital now!"

Nash hurried, but a train blocked their path and Evan Davis McGrath was born at the corner of Evans and Market with only his father and Mike Davis from the Marathon filling station in attendance. Mike said it was a quite a way to become someone's godfather.

Sitting in the loamy soil of her garden remembering the day Evan was born, Early decided she might as well laugh. In all truth, she'd laughed more in her thirty years with Nash than she'd cried, so it came naturally enough. Besides, it wasn't as though they were mad at each other or their feelings were hurt. That was part of their problem; their feelings for each other didn't seem to go deep enough anymore to be hurt.

"Girl, you look a little mindless sitting there in the radishes and the green onions laughing at nothing."

"Not the first time, now, is it?" She slanted a smile at her father-in-law. "Did you want something, Ben?"

"Thought maybe you'd feel like a walk." He grinned back at her, the expression crooked and irresistible and exactly like the ones his sons turned on people at the slightest provocation. "If you can make it as far as Donna's Diamond Dairy, I might be coerced into springing for an ice cream."

"Two dips?"

His nod propelled her to her feet with an inward sigh. The knees that had supported her unflinchingly for forty-six years, through learning to ride a bicycle, roller skate, and lots of praying and repenting, tired a lot more quickly than they used to. That was all there was to it. She might have to break down and move furniture after all, unless she was willing to find those kneepads. She would put Nash's recliner in the garage, just set it smack in the middle of the spot where he used to park his SUV, and while she was at it, she'd shove the big television he was so fond of out there, too. Then she could rent the garage to someone whose life had caught a change-up and left him bereft of a remote control and his own oversized chair. He could use the melamine dishes, too, and keep soft drinks and sliced cheese in the little refrigerator the kids had used at college.

"You sure this is what you want?" Ben waited until they were closer to Donna's than to the house to ask.

Only the promise of two dips of strawberry cheesecake ice cream kept her from turning on her heel and heading back toward the gated entry of Canterbury Crossing. She walked in silence for a few minutes, not sure what to say to this man she'd loved all these many years.

"I'm not the one who left," she said evenly.

And all of a sudden, standing in line at an ice cream stand with her father-in-law, the pain was overwhelming, and Early was in tears. Not quiet, dignified weeping that would befit the soon-to-be ex-wife of a prominent doctor, but great, gulping sobs that left her face splotchy and the front of Ben's shirt a wet mess.

"Come on, sugar. Sit down. Just wait there for me there."

They sat at a picnic table, dishes of ice cream between them. "He's feeling his age, Early," Ben said. "It happens to all of us, one time or another, in one way or another."

"Oh, really?" Her eyes felt as though someone had stuck lit matches into them. "You?"

He hesitated, sadness crossing his face in a wave. "Me."

"What did Rosie do?"

"Threw me out. Told me to come back when I was ready to be a grownup. Called me a couple of names she'd have washed the boys' mouths out with soap for using."

"I can see her doing that." Early smiled, the expression for once easy, not requiring conscious thought. "I've wished she was here so often lately, just for me. How's that for selfish?"

"I do it every day of my life."

By the time they'd finished their ice cream, Early felt soothed, certain she could survive another day. "Thank you." She slipped her hand into the crook of Ben's elbow as they stepped from cement sidewalks to the pseudo-antique cobblestone ones of the subdivision.

He gave her hand a pat and hugged it against his side. "You're my favorite daughter."

They stopped three doors down from Early's house, commenting on the colors of paint workmen were applying to the tri-level across the street.

"They'd look grand on a Victorian," Ben observed, "but on that house, they just look like grape soda pop and baby poop." He eyed the residents of the house as they worked in the flowers that lined their driveway. "Can we sit just a minute? It's getting hot."

Something in his voice alerted Early, and she glanced sharply at him. He'd lost color, and the skin of his arm was turning clammy right under her hand.

It was seventy-one degrees and not the slightest bit humid. A mild spring day.

"Ben?"

"Ah, Rosie," he muttered. "My arm hurts."

When he collapsed, his weight nearly took Early to the ground with him. "Oh, please, God," she said, straining to lower him gently. "Sweet Jesus, please. Ben, no. Don't you die on me. Don't you do it."

Kneeling in the soft new grass of one of Canterbury Crossing's most manicured lawns, Early looked around wildly. Surely someone would see them. She thought of the cell phone Nash was always urging her to carry. She'd finally consented to keeping it in her car, where it certainly didn't do any good right now.

"We called 911." The voice, breathless, came from above her. "Does he have a history of heart trouble?" One of the women who'd been working in her flowers knelt beside them, a trowel still in her hand.

"Only having it broken." Early hugged Ben's shoulders, as though he would be safe as long as her arms were around him. She prayed silently, desperately. She was out of practice, but the Lord still listened. Surely He did.

It seemed to take forever, but it was only minutes later that the wailing ambulance pulled under the porte-cochere of the hospital's emergency room.

Nash approached, a lab coat over his jeans and cotton sweater. He stayed out of the way of emergency room personnel. His face was grim, his brown eyes dark behind his glasses. Behind him came Evan, the third doctor in his father's family practice, whose Dockers, white shirt, and tie had become as much a uniform as Nash's jeans.

"What was he doing, Mom?" asked Evan, skidding to a stop. "Did he say anything?"

Early repeated Ben's words, seeing Nash's flinch out of the corner of her eye. "He hasn't regained consciousness," she said.

Tell me he's going to wake up, or if he's not, tell me he's with Rosie at least in his mind. Don't leave me swinging out here thinking it's somehow all my fault.

But they didn't tell her anything. Nash didn't even meet her eyes before he pushed his way through the doors into the emergency room. Evan hesitated a moment, then waved Early toward the waiting room before following his father's flapping white coat.

Someone in a pink smock brought her a cup of coffee, and she sipped greedily. As the wife of one doctor and the mother of another, she should probably don a pink smock more often herself.

Except that she wasn't a doctor's wife any longer, she remembered, the coffee turning bitter on her tongue. Ben wasn't the nearest thing to a father she had. She was no longer entitled to that proprietary little twinge she felt when other women looked at her husband. Her children were grown, professionals all. No one needed Early McGrath for anything. She was free.

Freedom.

She'd dreamed of it often, while getting Nash through medical school, raising babies, and caring for Rosie through those dark last days, but dreaming of it and having it were two different things.

By the time Evan emerged from behind the swinging doors, Early was on her third cup of coffee and had straightened the magazine racks twice.

"It was a bad one," he said. "It's a good thing he was with you. He probably wouldn't have made it if he'd been on his own. They'll do surgery in the morning. He'll be comfortable through the night, though."

Early sighed a silent prayer of thanksgiving and pleading. "How's your dad doing?"

"Cranky as ever." Evan grinned at her and accepted a cup of coffee from the woman in the pink smock with a nod of thanks. "Between him and Granddad, the air was turning blue in there, what with all the complaining. The ER nurses were teasing Granddad, telling him they understood now why Dad was such a crab, so then naturally both of them set about being charming. By the time I came out here, the whole staff was in love with Grand-dad, and of course, they're already crazy about Dad."

He got to his feet. "I'm going back to the office. Tell Dad he doesn't need to—I'll clear any paths with bumps left in them on his schedule."

It was Thursday, Nash's half-day day off. Early wondered why they even bothered with non-scheduled time, since the R and R never actually came to pass. She wished she had a dollar for every time she'd been left waiting for Nash's promised timely arrival.

Left waiting. Must be the story of a doctor's wife, just as freedom was the story of the ex-wife.

The volunteer had made a fresh pot of coffee, and Early was on her second cup of it when Nash materialized in front of her. "Come on," he said. "I'll run you home."

"Okay." She laid her hand in his, allowing him to help her to her feet.

At her behest, Nash stopped at a supermarket, and she bought a bouquet of roses for the neighbors who called 911 and sat with Early and Ben those desperate five minutes until the ambulance came. "Just stop and run in," she said. "Or I can."

"We both can," he said. "He may be my father, but he likes you better than he does me."

She didn't respond to the old joke. Her line was, "Sure, but I'm a better cook," and she'd said it a hundred times since it had ceased being funny. She didn't have the emotional strength to make it a hundred and one. She was angry, and it was taking all she had to stay that way.

"I'm worried about him." Nash pulled into what used to be their driveway after they'd dropped off the flowers with thanks for the neighborliness that had been extended. "He's always been healthy as a horse."

"He will be again." She looked over at him. "Won't he?"

"I hope so. He's been at loose ends without Mama. I thought moving him up here would give him something to live for, being close to us and the kids, but it hasn't. The ends are looser than ever, and I'm afraid he doesn't care if he lives or not."

"So let him move back home when he gets out of the hospital," she said. "You and Joe can afford care for him until he gets back on his feet. For that matter, he can afford it for himself. You can go down on alternate weekends, especially since you're both single. The kids will always go to visit their grandfather, no matter where he is." She opened her door without looking at him again.

"I'll walk you in."

Don't! If you come in, you'll see me cry over your father and you'll try to make me feel better. Then I'll end up offering to move down to the country with him because I've already been thinking that would be the easiest thing for everyone else. And I'm tired of doing the easiest thing for everyone else. Tired! Do you hear me?

Oh, good grief, of course he didn't hear her. Mind reading was the responsibility of the wife part of a marriage, not the husband one. The husband didn't even have to listen to the spoken word. He just had to grunt often enough to show he was still alive.

But Nash checked the house with all the impersonality of a bored police officer, told her he'd see her later and to take care now, and left.

Early dropped clothes all the way to the bathroom and stepped under a stinging shower.

And that was when she cried.

NASH RELEASED A RELIEVED SIGH. EARLY LOOKED SO SAD WHEN he left that he was afraid she was going to cry. Even if he wasn't in love with his ex-wife anymore, even if he wasn't sure he ever had been, he didn't like seeing her cry. She didn't cry pretty, for one thing, with glistening eyes and tears hanging like diamonds from her lashes. No, Early cried noisy and splotchy.

For another thing, even if she was crying over his father today, Nash was fairly certain his departure from their marriage and their home was at the root of it. He felt guilty, and he didn't like the feeling a bit.

And then there was the third thing. Beyond fairly, he was *absolutely* certain if Early had cried, he'd have cried with her.

At the apartment complex where he rented a two-bedroom-two-bath in the same building that housed Joe, his thrice-divorced brother, and Evan, who enjoyed his bachelorhood to an extent that horrified Early, Nash left a message with his brother's secretary and stepped into the shower. He let the spray wash lukewarm over him and leaned against the wall.

This was probably what Early had done when he left; she always cried in the shower. It was, she informed him, how she'd survived raising four children and one husband.

"Every one of your kids was here," Ben grumbled when Early entered his room later in the day. "Don't they have jobs?"

"Shoot, no. They think you're going to kick off and leave them a fortune." Early hoisted herself onto the edge of his bed and scowled at him. "Don't you even consider it. They need to work for a living."

"Jessie did ask me if my will was up to date. Offered to change it free of charge if I'd make it worth her while in the long run." In the tired face that seemed more lined than it had been at the ice cream stand earlier in the day, Ben's brown eyes still laughed.

"That's Joe's fault. He's the one who talked her into law school and hired her as soon as she graduated. Has he been here?"

"Yeah, he came with Jess. Always on the run, that boy is. Soon as he figures out what he's running from, he might settle down. Don't think I'll hold my breath for that to happen, though, seeing as how he's forty-five and no closer than he was twenty years and three wives ago."

"I know Logan and Anna came by." Early named her second son and his wife. "I watched the kids, and they helped me plant carrots. Whole pack of seeds went in one little spot. It'll look like a big fern growing there."

"Sarah had a black eye when she came," Ben reported. "One of her kids didn't take kindly to something. Never knew special education would be such a violent field."

"She was prepared, being the youngest in the house. She fought for everything, whether she needed to or not." Early looked at her watch. "I think I better go and let you get some rest. It'll be a big day tomorrow, and you're going to feel lousy for most of it." *Besides, I know Nash will stop in, and I can't see him again today. I just can't.*

Ben caught her hand. "I don't like to be a baby, especially at the ripe old age of seventy," he said, "but would you stay awhile?" His chuckle caught in his throat. "I'm afraid Jessie will come in and force the issue about my will."

"Sure." She didn't have to think about it. Ben McGrath seldom asked her for so much as the time of her day. When he did ask, she was going to respond. She kissed his cheek. "Rest, handsome. I'll be right here."

Early had missed enough sleep during the time of having four teenagers in the house that she still felt as though she was catching up; therefore, if it was dark and she was even close to lying down, she fell asleep. This night, with her hand resting lightly on her father-in-law's, was no exception.

Her eyes opened once when a blanket floated over her. "Sh," Nash whispered. "Just sleep."

She woke at five, as she usually did. Nash was asleep in a chair on the other side of the bed. His hair was a dark brown mess, his glasses still on his face but askew. She had, she realized, slept better in a fake leather recliner with him in the room than she had since he'd left home.

How many nights had they spent together in hospital rooms in thirty years? With each hospitalization of each child. When Early had a miscarriage early on, a hysterectomy just a few years ago. When Nash had his gall bladder removed in his thirties. His angioplasty last year. They'd always been relieved to get back home and into their own bed. Somehow, she thought that relief would escape her this time.

"Are you going to observe?" she asked Nash later, after kissing Ben and watching the gurney roll onto the elevator.

"No. Evan is, so he'll keep us posted." Nash yawned widely. "Let's go get some coffee."

She went home after having coffee with Nash, reflecting that the house in Canterbury Crossing got lonelier every time she walked into it. She went out back to plant the flats of flowers that had been waiting patiently beside the door.

While she was at it, she dug up the carrots. She didn't like them either.

CHAPTER 2

"He just wants to go home, back to the Ridge. Early, has he been that unhappy up here?" Joe looked at her.

Early refilled the iced tea glasses that sat on the table and went back around the counter to sit on a barstool and rip stitches out of an appliquéd quilt block. If she separated herself from those who had been born as or were still married to McGraths, surely they wouldn't expect her to do the things they didn't want to, would they?

"He's been lonely, Joe. You know that." Nash's voice was impatient, as it usually was when he spoke to his younger brother. "Good heavens, he and Mama were closer than two coats of paint for forty years. I don't think he realizes he'd have been lonely on the Ridge, too."

"Well, he can't go back there and live by himself," said Evan. "He'll come back from this surgery, but he'll still bear watching. If he's left on his own, he'll be living on a diet comprised mainly of trans-fats and carbohydrates and smoking his pipe all day long. His idea of exercise will be thumbing the remote control." His grin was wicked and familiar when he looked at his father. "Kind of like yours, Dad."

"He could stay with us," said Logan, exchanging a silent message with his wife.

Early looked at her daughter-in-law and saw her wide smile of agreement and her nod.

"Of course he can," Anna said. "We could make him an apartment out of one side of the garage so he could have privacy and some respite from the kids' noise."

Anna, you can't. Logan will mean to help, but he won't. Jessie and Sarah will mean to stop by more often, but they won't. Say no, honey. But Anna couldn't hear her thoughts, couldn't know after six years of marriage what Early had learned in thirty.

Early laid down the quilt block.

"I can come by more often, Anna, to give you a break," Jessie offered.

"Me, too," said Sarah, "especially after school's out."

Nash nodded thoughtfully. "It might work."

Early looked across the counter, over the children's heads, searching to meet his eyes. *No, it won't, Nash. What's wrong with you?*

"Excuse me." Oh, phooey. What was it with her that she couldn't manage to keep her mouth shut? "You're all talking as though Ben is unable to think or speak for himself. Is this some new development since I saw him yesterday, when he was flirting outrageously with the nurses and trying to talk his way into going home early?"

"He's not especially trustworthy at taking care of himself," Nash said. "That's how he got into this mess to start with."

"Oh?" She hiked an eyebrow at him. "So speaketh Dr. Angioplasty himself? Remember that, children, if your father has further problems with his heart. Just chuck him into a home and visit him once a week."

"Well, fine, Mrs. Knows-all," snapped Nash. "What do you suggest?"

"Make that *ex*-Mrs. Knows-More-Than-You-Think, if it's all the same to you," she said crisply. "I suggest you remember that Ben is a grownup and treat him with the dignity he's earned."

"That's not an answer."

"Well, then, why don't you and Joe go down to the Ridge and see what you can find? There's sure to be someone who would check on him on a daily basis. We grew up there. It's not as if he wants to move into a nest of rattlesnakes or strangers."

Her sensible inner voice interrupted. *Don't offer to do it for them. You're done taking care of people.*

"I'm going down to see Mother today. I can check around." So much for sensible inner voices. Early raised her eyebrow again. "Anyone who wants to is welcome to come along. I'm sure your grandmother would be delighted to see you."

"Excuse me, Mama, but I don't think Granny Fran has ever been delighted about anything in her whole life." Jessie got to her feet. "This has been just the most fun, but I need to stop by the office and then go home and try to look like a real girl." She fluttered her considerable eyelashes at her brothers. "I have a date."

"I have to go, too." Sarah threw Early an apologetic look. "I'm sorry I can't go to Gran's with you."

"It's all right, sweetie." Early kissed the girls as they left. "Drive carefully."

"Do everything carefully." Nash kissed them, too. He gave his brother a look of disgust that turned to a smile when his gaze moved on to Anna and Logan. "It's nice of you two, but as much as it grieves me to agree with your mother, she's right. Your granddad can't be pushed around like that, nor should he be. And you two have enough on your plate, with the little ones and your job, Logan, and nursing school, Anna."

Within ten minutes, everyone was gone but Nash. Early gathered sweaty glasses and tried to talk herself out of being pleased that he'd agreed with her about something of substance.

She wasn't pleased about everything, though. She frowned at him when he plucked her keys from her hand. "You don't have to go with me. And even if you do, you're not driving. My car doesn't like you, and I'm not all that fond of you these days myself." Driving fifty-seven miles into the country with a back-seat driver didn't thrill her at all—turning her keys over to him was untenable. Especially since the ink hadn't even dried on their divorce decree yet.

"I don't mind. I should check on Fran anyway and take her some samples." He grinned cheerfully, though his eyes darkened. "'Sides that, you know full well she's going to blame you up, down, and sideways for this divorce. I need to set her straight on that one." He squirted dishwashing liquid into the sink and ran hot water into it.

Early got a dry dishtowel out of the drawer and stood for a minute, looking so hard at the apple-bedecked terrycloth that the colors blurred.

She had to ask. She didn't want to—she just had to.

"Are you happy, Nash, now that you're alone?" She corrected herself hurriedly. "Well, now that you're not with me, anyway. I don't know if you're alone or not." *And I don't care.*

I don't. Really.

Which was good, because he didn't answer her question, just told her the window over the sink needed to be re-caulked even though the house was nearly brand new.

THE RIDGE INCLUDED THE TOWN OF PLEASANT HILL, WHICH boasted the community school, a strip mall on either end of town, and the hospital; the four-corners community with the unlikely name of Four Corners and a church that had been called the little church at the Corners for so long no one could remember if it had another name; Stringtown Proper, which had recently become the home of the area's only Wal-Mart and as a consequence had also gained its own medical clinic, liquor store, and municipal swimming pool; and Over Yonder, where decent folk took care not to go—leastways not during daylight when anyone could see them. The four settlements were connected by hills and hollers and gravel roads that were supposed to be two lanes but really only worked that way if one of the vehicles was a bicycle and the other a compact car. Or else you could drive all the way around the outside of them on the Ridge Parkway, a four-lane road with exits for each municipality and the interstate.

In the olden, golden days of Nash's youth, there had been an elementary school in each town, with fierce rivalries between the communities over which one was best. Come seventh grade, however, everyone got on buses and rode through the hollers to Pleasant Hill and went to the melting pot that was Ridge Consolidated Junior-Senior High School. There was lots of fraternization, and before you knew it, you had Four Corners girls dating Stringtown Proper boys.

Nowadays, the campus in Pleasant Hill included an elementary building and a playground and the whole thing was named Ridge Community Schools. It was better, most everyone agreed, at least till the hollers filled up with snow and your kids were stuck home for three days running.

Francie Winslow, Early's mother, lived in a little two-bedroom ranch house in Pleasant Hill. Nash had bought it for her when it came to his attention that you could see daylight through the floorboards of her kitchen in Four Corners. This was how it came to be that, although Francie had little patience with her daughter, she completely adored him.

"You could put your daddy in the nursing home over to the other side of town," she suggested. "It's a nice enough place, and I think they got most of those violations took care of."

Early, who Francie had put to work cleaning the tops of the cupboards, tossed him a furious look.

"I don't think so, Fran," Nash said easily. "You may not be afraid of my dad, but I am. He'd hurt me real bad if I even suggested such a thing." When Early snorted, he grinned at her. "If Early didn't kill me first, that is."

"'Course, he still owns his house up the mountain 'tween Stringtown and Four Corners," said Francie thoughtfully. "It's way too big for one person, though, and isn't it rented out?"

"Not right now." Nash sipped his coffee. "Has been, though, to its detriment."

"You can't hardly see it from the road since the trees are leafed out, and there's no telling what kind of condition renters have left it in." Francie got up from the table. "Now, you get those corners real good, Earline. I swear, cobwebs just grow right up before your very eyes if you're not careful."

"Yes, ma'am." Early glared at the back of her mother's head.

"So how are all the children?" Francie refilled Nash's cup. "Anna's not pregnant again, is she? Land's sake, Earline, she must be as fertile as you. I thought for a while you and Nash were going to have a baby every year, then you were saddled with Sarah on top of that," Francie fussed.

Nash tried not to grimace, but Early stiffened and stopped cleaning.

"Sarah was a gift from God." Early's voice dripped ice, the cleaning cloth hanging from her hand. "Just as her mother was."

She'd never been one for throwing things—Nash prayed she wouldn't start now.

Flame climbed up Francie's rouged cheeks. "Susan was a punishment for sins both real and imagined. Sarah is an extension of that punishment."

"Sarah is our fourth child, Francie," Nash said quietly, "and, as her mother said, a gift for which we are grateful every day. You done up there, Early? Why don't we go take a look at Mama and Dad's house?"

"You didn't answer my questions," said Francie, seemingly oblivious to Early's fury. "About the children. Is Anna pregnant or not? Is Evan ever going to get married? Jessie's not still hanging around that Walden boy from Pleasant Hill, is she? He's bad news, mark my words."

Early climbed down from the chair. "Anna's not pregnant, though it's her own business if she is. Jessie's sort of dating a lawyer who looks like Ryan Gosling. We can only hope for the female population of Lexington that Evan's not considering marriage—he'd be a terrible husband. And not that you asked, but Sarah's fine."

Francie ran an arthritic finger along the edge of one of the cupboards Early had waxed, checking it for cleanliness. "Not dating, though, even though she's twenty-five and not bad looking. Bad blood shows, mark my words, and decent men won't have anything to do with her."

Early opened her mouth, but Nash gripped her arm, and she closed it again.

"We'll be back later, Francie," he said. "Be ready about seven, and we'll take you to supper."

Regardless of her stance on his driving, she didn't object when he took the keys from her hand and opened the passenger door for her. "I'm afraid you'll drive us into a wall," he said. "You have to stop letting her get you so upset, Early."

"She would upset anyone, so don't blame me," she said sharply. "If she were your mother, you'd be upset, too. Look at the effect Joe has on you and all he does is marry the wrong people."

He snorted. "Joe's a forty-five-year-old adolescent."

"Mother's a sixty-six-year-old termagant. Wanna trade?"

"Doesn't matter. We married each other, and part of it was that you got my brother and I got your mother. Even in the divorce, there are no givebacks of the relatives."

They drove along in silence, the car whispering through the curves toward Stringtown Proper. "Nash, why did you do it?" Early asked. "I know I've asked before, probably five times since you left, but you've never given a good reason. Why did you want a divorce?"

Nash looked over at her. From any other spurned wife, that question probably would have sounded pathetic. But it didn't from Early; her voice was calm, dry, matter-of-fact, just as it always was. For a moment, he knew sheer terror. Did a divorce mean she wouldn't be in his life anymore except in the satellite function of being his kids' mother?

"You're my best friend, Early," he said.

"Well, that's certainly a good reason."

He thought for a minute, trying to put words together that matched the emotions raging inside him. "It is when that's all you are."

The swift intake of her breath told him he'd hurt her. "I'm sorry," he said. "I didn't want to—"

"It's all right." She was looking out the passenger window and he couldn't see her face, but the pain seemed to arc between them. "I asked for it."

EVERY TIME EARLY WALKED INTO THE HOUSE WHERE NASH HAD grown up, she fell in love with it. Today was no exception.

It was a terrible mess. No one had scoured the toilets in what appeared to be years, the last tenants had taken the kitchen appliances when they left, and there were nearly as many spindles missing from the banister on the open stairway as remained.

"It's way too much for Dad," Nash said.

Don't say it, Early. You're done being the caretaker. "But not for him and me." *Well, you thought you were. You and your big mouth.*

"You're crazy."

Maybe she was, but she didn't need him telling her so. Early stuck out her chin belligerently. "Why?"

"Early, your life's in Lexington. The kids are in Lexington. *I'm* in Lexington." He smiled unkindly and played his trump card. "Your mother's here."

"She's clear across the Ridge. If there's snow on the ground, she may as well be in Lexington."

"This is the first week of May, Early. By the time there's snow on the ground, Francie will have driven you over the edge."

"Would I have enough money after we sell our house to buy this one from Ben, pay someone for repairs, and maybe build on more downstairs bedrooms?"

He sighed. "Yes. Pay for it and probably put a pool out back. But, Early, what will you *do* if you move down here? I don't know how to break this to you, but this is a depressed area. There are no jobs, no universities, and not much market for someone who can sew pretty quilts and make African violets grow anywhere."

"Well, you know what?" she said, holding her eyes wide so they wouldn't tear up like she was a teenager with hurt feelings. She was a middle-aged woman with hurt feelings, which was entirely different. "There's not much market in Canterbury Crossing for fat and frumpy forty-six-year-old divorcees who never finished high school, either."

He came around the end of the counter and put his hands on her cheeks, the touch a caress she longed to lean into.

"You'll be living Francie Winslow's life," he said. "Is that what you want?"

She kept her eyes steady on his with an effort. More than one woman patient had fallen silent and mesmerized under that warm gaze, and Early was no less susceptible for having known him longer and better than any of them. "What I wanted," she said softly, "was to live Early McGrath's life, but it's been taken away from me, hasn't it?" She withdrew from his hands. "When can Ben and I move in?"

CHAPTER 3

Even though she and Nash had lived separately for several months by the time she moved into the house in Stringtown Proper, she couldn't sleep. Early had grown somewhat accustomed to sleeping alone—as long as she had plenty of pillows on the other side of the bed—but it had been many years since she'd lived in the country.

It was quiet.

Not the pleasant but manufactured quiet of a central air conditioning unit, although the house had one, nor the sound of television or music played low. Not even the white noise hum of the refrigerator, since the kitchen was some distance from her bedroom.

Just quiet.

Unable to sleep, she made coffee and carried it and her phone to the back porch, sat on the glider and propped her feet in a chair. This was aloneness far different from what she'd felt in Canterbury Crossing, just as the quiet was—well, to tell the truth, it wasn't quiet at all.

Little Cat Creek wandered through the trees that backed the

property, and she could hear the water slapping against rocks and the snorts of deer—at least, she hoped it was deer—as they drank. Frogs ribbeted and ducks quacked and leaves whispered against each other in mysterious night music.

The sounds were alien, yet achingly familiar at the same time. She and Susie used to play in the other end of Little Cat where it flowed behind the rickety little house over at Four Corners. High school boys dammed up a place and made it wide and deep enough for swimming, and they spent hours there. For all her limitations, Susie swam beautifully, looking like a small blonde sprite in the water while dumpy and dun-colored Early plodded to keep up.

Later on, when Susie sneaked away from the house, Little Cat was always the first place Early looked for her. She could still remember Nash's shock.

"The water? She goes around the water? Early, isn't she...uh...slow?"

"In her mind, she is," Early said, glad it was dark so he couldn't see her embarrassment. "But swimming-wise, she's way too fast for me. She's still a physical adult."

Susan grew up in other ways, too, and was attractive to boys despite her disabilities. Early worried constantly.

"We can keep her with us more, protect her that way," Nash promised.

But they hadn't even protected themselves, much less Early's mentally-challenged older sister, and when Nash went to Lexington on his scholarship, Early moved in with Ben and Rosie to await the birth of their baby. Nash came home weekends to work at Waylon's, where Early sat on empty pallets and helped him with his homework.

Evan was five, Logan three, and Jessica barely walking when Susie gave frightened and bewildered birth to a tiny girl. No one,

Susie least of all, had any idea who little Sarah Earline's father was.

When the baby was six months old, Susie came up missing one last time. Early and Nash found her in the creek again, only this time she wasn't swimming. White-faced, Nash took off his shirt and handed it to Early to cover Susie. "Go get someone," he told her hoarsely, but Early shook her head, sitting on the ground and rocking her dead sister in her arms.

"Turn your eyes upon Jesus," she sang in a broken, crooning voice, "look full in His wonderful face..."

Nash had to leave her to go for help. Years later, remembering, Early realized how difficult that had been for him, that he carried the horror of that day in his soul just as she did but in an entirely different way. Raised traditionally, he'd felt he should be able to protect his wife from pain and loss; on that day, he'd known irrevocably that he could not.

Susan Winslow's death at the age of twenty-four was ruled an accident. A welfare representative came from the county seat to take Sarah with her, but Early scooped her niece into her arms and said that wouldn't be either necessary or tolerated. Her gaze had been on Nash's, even as her mother sputtered protests and the social worker voiced objections.

"We are her family." Nash took the baby and stood tall beside his wife. "Who else will tell her that her mother swam like a mermaid and looked like an angel and that she loved Sarah as well as she could?"

After almost six years of marriage, that was the day Early had known beyond all doubt that she was in love with her husband.

Leaning back in her patio chair, sipping her coffee, she wondered when and if she had fallen out of love with him, when the relationship had become merely comfortable. Boring. She guessed, truth be told, she should be grateful to Nash for having the courage to end it, to say, "I think we need to get a divorce."

She *should* be grateful, maybe, but she wasn't. She liked being married, liked being the matriarch when the house filled with kids and grandkids and noise. For that matter, she liked Nash. He was her best friend. But he'd said that wasn't enough and, even though hearing it had hurt like little else she'd ever experienced, he was probably right.

A breeze floated through the porch, ruffling the white knit of her nightgown and waking the loneliness she was still trying to get used to. She wondered, not for the first time, if finding someone else had been the catalyst for Nash's departure. He'd said not, but that wasn't something most husbands were truthful about, as far as she knew. She found it disturbing that even six months after the separation and with the divorce final, the idea of Nash with someone else was devastating.

She picked up the phone. She would call Evan first, she decided, and leave a message so that he would call her back in his own time. He was never home. Then Logan and Anna, then the girls. She'd never before realized that she always phoned them in order of birth—kind of like calling them in to supper when they were kids.

But when she punched in the memory dial of the phone, it was Nash who answered. "Are you busy?" she asked.

"Not too busy to talk to you," he answered. "Let me go outside. I don't need my dad eavesdropping when I'm talking to a girl. I think I'm a bit beyond that."

"You're just afraid he'll ground you."

"You bet." His sigh was deep. He sounded tired. "How's it going, Early?"

"Fine. The stuff's all done inside the house, and Noah Walden and his dad are going to start on the outside tomorrow. I'll bring Ben some carpet samples to look at." She hesitated. "Are the kids all okay?"

"Yes, every one of them. Homesick, are you?"

The gentle mockery in his voice made her want to sniffle. "A little bit," she admitted. "I like being back down here, but I kind of wish everyone else was here, too, at least part of the time."

"They'll be down over the weekend, making so much noise and mess you'll be wishing them away again."

"Probably." Although she never did. She missed the noise and mess nearly as much as she missed the people who created it.

Silence fell between them, heavy and not quite comfortable. She didn't know what she wanted him to say, but he wasn't saying it. Early clutched the phone and thought of how often in their lives that had happened. How many times had she waited to hear the right words only to be disappointed? What in the world had kept them together for thirty years if they couldn't even communicate on the simplest level?

"Well," she said, "I'd better go. Goodnight, Nash." *Now, there, that's communication. Idiot.*

"Sleep warm, Early."

"You, too."

She disconnected the phone, but kept it close to her ear, as though she could still hear the sound of his voice as it said the wrong things.

There had been times, though. She smiled into the darkness.

"Your eyes remind me of spring rain. They're so light gray and clear. Warm and cool at the same time and sometimes when I'm holding you they get downright hot, like a thunderstorm in April."

Logan had been a newborn when Nash said that, and she'd held the words as close to her heart as she did the baby. If they couldn't always have love—and Early was the first to admit they hadn't always—they'd had poetry in the night and the most beautiful children.

When had the poetry died and the words dried up?

And why did she keep listening?

My dad came along to help you paint trim, Miss Early. I told him you weren't any too quick at it." Noah Walden grinned at her.

She narrowed her gaze at him, the boy Francie swore was bad news. His eyes were crystalline green, bright and laughing as they met hers. "Young man, I have grounded my children for less."

"No, you haven't," he said. "Once you found out grounding meant you were stuck in the house with them, you gave it up." He nodded, owl-like. "I know these things."

She raised helpless hands. "Nothing is sacred."

"You know this younger generation." A man she assumed to be Noah's father stepped around him and extended his hand. "Josh Walden. It's been a good many years, but I do believe your husband and I created a little discontent here and there along the Ridge in our salad days. Being younger and entirely innocent, you probably don't remember."

Early laughed. "That and the fact that we Four Corners girls were taught to stay away from Stringtown boys—not that we did, mind you. I'm happy to see you, especially if you've come to paint trim. I truly hate it."

"I teach over at the high school, and yesterday was the last day of school. Noah's afraid I'll get into trouble if I don't stay busy."

"Nah." Noah left them, heading toward the living room, the last room to be finished. "He just works cheap," he called over his shoulder. "Offer him some coffee, ma'am, and he'll be your friend for life."

Early smiled at Josh. "You sound just like a puppy."

"Housebroken and all."

He painted the trim on the porch while she stretched a quilt onto Rosie's old frame and sat down with her threaded needles. They worked comfortably, the classic rock music on her playlist working as a conversation catalyst.

"Noah says you're divorced."

"Yes." She clipped the word off the way she always did. She still considered the breakdown of her marriage a personal failure she didn't like to discuss. She pushed the needle in and out, in and out.

"I'm sorry." He met her gaze over the top of the quilting frame. "I imagine it's very hard after this long."

"Yes." She paused, feeling awkward. "I don't know what to do, you know. It's like I've defined myself as Nash's wife and the kids' mother for so long that if there's another person inside, I can't find her."

"It was like that when my wife Jackie died," he said, "and I felt betrayed, mad at her for a while, because we'd made all these plans, and then she just left me. Then I was mad at myself for being mad at her."

"It's one of the stages of grief."

"I know that now. Maybe, at some level, I knew it then, but all I understood was that I was alone and I didn't want to be and I was angry about it."

Early nodded. "I can identify with that. How long has it been?"

"A little over two years." He shook his head, his gaze far away. "Sometimes it still feels like yesterday."

"Was your wife from here?"

"Michigan, and that's where we lived till ten years ago or so. I met her in college. She was working at McDonald's and when she brought me a vanilla shake, she spilled it all over me. I knew right away it was love."

Early laughed. "I'm a McDonald's alumna, too. I worked there most of the time Nash was in college and med school. He'd come down with the babies and study while I worked. Everyone in McDonald's, including regular customers, helped take care of Evan and Logan."

She paused, focusing on the trees behind the house. She'd forgotten how hard they'd both worked and how much fun they'd had. When Nash had graduated from UK, they'd had his party at McDonald's.

"Good times, I'll bet." Josh's voice was quiet, his paintbrush still.

She started, having forgotten he was there. "Yes," she said just as quietly. "More coffee?"

"Please."

When he left that evening, wearing considerably less paint on his person than Early did when she tackled painting, he paused at the door. "Dinner Friday night? Not McDonald's."

"That would be nice. Thank you."

"Seven?"

She nodded.

"No, you can't date. Mothers don't date. That's all there is to it." Jessie's voice crackled over the phone, and Early imagined sparks shooting from her Nash-brown eyes.

She sighed, scrunching the receiver between her ear and her shoulder while she applied "Afternoon Delite" polish to her acrylic-enhanced fingernails. "Now tell me something, Jessica Darcy, would you be this upset if your father asked you about the legalities of dating or if I weren't going out with Noah Walden's father?"

"Noah has nothing to do with anything."

"Too bad. He's a nice boy."

"Who'll never come off the Ridge. He's made that completely clear to me."

"So?" Early smudged a nail. "Drat it."

Jessie's voice was long-suffering now. "Mama, you and Daddy always made it plain you wanted us to do better."

"Better than what?"

"Than you did."

"Excuse me? I don't think we did so badly."

"No, but you didn't want Sarah and me dropping three babies before we were twenty-one. You used to worry when we spent time with Granddad and Grandma Rosie because you were afraid we'd get too close with boys from the Ridge."

"We were afraid you'd get too close with anyone, not just boys from the Ridge." That wasn't strictly true, but Early had no intention of admitting it, especially since she'd been completely wrong. "And the term 'dropping babies' is a real misnomer, because it's nowhere near that easy."

"So Sarah and I thought we'd come down this weekend and help you finish up Granddad's room. Is that okay?" Jessie sniffed audibly and rudely. "Is there time in your active social life?"

"Oh, I'll make time for you girls," Early said cheerfully. "When will you be here?"

"Saturday. I have a date Friday night and Sarah's fixing dinner for Granddad." Jessie hesitated. "Something's bothering her, by the way, but I don't know what it is. She's so quiet it worries me."

"She's always quiet, honey." *And we always worry about her.* Even though the words remained unspoken, Early knew Jessie felt them, and for a moment there was close and warm accord between them. "I love you, Jess."

"Me, too, Mama. See you Saturday."

Early poured more coffee, polished the nails on her right hand, and called Sarah as she stepped onto the porch.

"Hi, baby," she said to her younger daughter's voicemail. "Jessie says you're coming down this weekend. I'll be glad to see you. Love you."

She waited, just a few seconds, to see if Sarah would pick up, but she didn't. She hardly ever did.

The phone in her hand rang as soon as she'd disconnected, and she jumped, spilling her coffee down the side of one leg.

"Hello!"

"Oops. What did you spill?"

"Coffee. Almost hot." She would not allow herself to feel the pleasure Nash's voice created, nor would she give credence to the thought that she'd be able to sleep tonight—the only thing better than talking to him would be if he was there with her. Just till she got to sleep, of course.

"Your daughter—" She cleared her throat and tried again. "Your daughter is a pain in the neck."

"I don't even have to ask which one," he said, and their laughter rolled between them like coins on a wood floor, falling against each other in a musical jingle. "What's Jess done now?"

"Oh, nothing." She wasn't ready to talk to Nash about dating. If he was already picking up women in his SUV and taking them to dinner, she didn't want to know about it. "How's Ben?"

"Champing at the bit to get out of here. He can start rehab at the Stringtown clinic next week, so whenever you're ready, we can move him." He sighed. "Are you sure you want to do this, Early?"

"Do you have any viable alternatives?"

"Not really."

"Have you talked to Sarah lately?"

"Dad has. I've talked to her voicemail. Who set that up for her anyway? "

"Evan. Since she lives alone, he was worried about weird

guys calling her and he wanted her to screen her calls. I guess you're just one of the weird guys."

"Uh-huh. And have you talked to her, since I'm too weird for her to pick up her phone?"

"No," Early admitted. "What did Ben say when he did?"

"That she was talking between the lines. If he asked her one question, she answered another. He said she seems happy enough, just evasive." His voice changed, although the alteration was subtle enough the listener would have had to have lived with him for thirty years to catch it. "How about you? You happy?"

Happy? Was he insane?

"The house is about done. It's really come out well. I hope Ben's pleased with it. Still thinking about a pool, if he'd like to have one. And Noah's working on designing a quilt shop for me. Not that I'll have the nerve to open it even when it's built."

"There's no hurry, is there?"

"No."

There was no hurry for anything, she reflected later, lying in bed and watching *Little Women,* the comforting one in which Katherine Hepburn portrayed Jo March. Life should have been a pleasure, a cozy segue into a relaxing middle age. And it *was* cozy, this room with a fireplace and the bed covered with quilts she'd made.

It was also boring. The thing with having nowhere you had to go, she was learning, was that you didn't care if you went anywhere. If there was no goal beyond getting into the car and driving around over the Ridge's two-lane roads and then coming back, what was the point?

The thought made her swing her feet to the floor and walk to the French doors that opened onto the upper deck. She undid the locks and stepped outside. The floorboards were smooth and cool under her feet, the night sounds muted as though the wildlife was finding its way to bed.

What is the point, Lord? What's the point of it all? Do You have plans for me You haven't let me in on yet?

How long had it been since she'd asked rather than forging ahead? She wasn't one of the "lucky shepherds" who heard the voice of God whenever she needed to. At least, she didn't think she was. Maybe she just hadn't been listening.

SHE WOKE, AS SHE ALWAYS DID, IN TIME TO TAKE HER COFFEE outside and watch the sun bounce up from behind Over Yonder Mountain. The dew sparkled on her tomato plants and the rainbow slashes of the flower beds, and she wondered idly how her garden in Lexington was doing since Logan's family had moved into the house. Anna and the children spent prodigious amounts of time in it.

"You raised your kids in the garden along with the vegetables, teaching them what was weeds and what was plants, and they grew straight and tall just like your produce did. I could do worse." Anna's eyes had glinted then, and she'd laughed. "Besides, Logan likes me grubby."

Logan liked his wife any old way at all, just the way she liked him. Early closed her eyes, breathing a little prayer of gratitude for this easy and lovely branch of her family tree.

From across Little Cat, she heard the crow of Reginald, Mary Brad Hardesty's pedigreed rooster, signaling a new day on the Ridge. Early realized that today was Wednesday, and in Lexington she would be hearing the beeping of the garbage truck as it made its cumbersome way through Canterbury Crossing. This had been her clue to start her morning walk, but never till the truck had gone past, as though its occupants would have been embarrassed by the sight of a slightly plump matron doing her

half-hour of cardio-vascular in faded sweats and a hat that advertised Stringtown Proper Feed & Seed.

She, like Reginald, who had come by express mail from
somewhere exotic like Indianapolis, had crossed the road, and
wasn't that then the point of it all?

To get to the other side.

Ah. Sometimes listening worked.

CHAPTER 4

"DATING'S NOT LIKE RIDING A BICYCLE, IS IT?" EARLY LOOKED from the jeans with more holes than denim in the legs to the top that exposed her navel and two stretch marks if she turned just so. What was it she'd read about dressing-room mirrors? How many pounds did they add?

"More like the Ferris wheel," Mary Brad admitted. "It was fun the first time but you'd just as soon not do it anymore." She frowned at the skin that kept popping over the waist of the jeans. "Tuck it in there, Early. You should consider lipo, you know, if you're going to get into this whole Ferris wheel thing."

Early emerged from the shirt she'd just pulled off over her head, scowling at her friend and neighbor. "I could have gone all day without hearing that." She replaced the shirt on its hanger and reached for the peach-colored cotton sweater that was next.

She turned sideways in front of the mirror to gaze at the short sleeved sweater. She raised her arms to see if it, too, exposed her stretch marks and the only female navel in the family aside from Francie's not graced with a small gold hoop. "This one isn't bad if I lose these jeans and wear my old faithful white pants."

"Works," Mary Brad agreed

Early chewed her bottom lip. "I haven't so much as kissed anyone but Nash since I was fifteen. Unless you count family members."

The other woman twitched the jeans into semi-neatness on their hanger. "Speaking of family members," she said, not looking at Early, "how's that useless brother of Nash's?"

"Pick up the phone sometime when he calls," Early suggested dryly. "You might find out."

"And then I could write me a book. *Heartbreak on the Ridge* by Mary Brad Hardesty."

"It has a ring to it." Early carried the sweater to the service counter, digging for her wallet.

EARLY HAD JUST STEPPED FROM THE SHOWER WHEN THE DOORBELL rang, pealing out the opening notes of the "William Tell Overture."

"Where are you when I need you, Tonto?" she muttered, dragging a robe over her wet skin and wrapping her hair into a towel. By the time she swung open the side-lighted door, she was breathless.

"Didn't I give you a key?" she said, brushing past Nash to hug her father-in-law. "Welcome home. I thought you were coming tomorrow, but I'm glad to see you anyway."

"We *were* coming tomorrow," Nash said, "but Jessie said tonight would be better. You did give me a key, but I didn't think I should use it indiscriminately. Go on in, Dad. She doesn't bite any harder than she ever did."

Early smiled at Ben and frowned at Nash. "When you talk to your daughter again, give her a time out. I suppose she's a little beyond spanking, not that it ever did any good anyway. And the key wasn't for you, it was for your dad. It's still his house, after all."

"Oh." Nash rummaged in the pocket of his khaki shorts and came up with a key. "Here you go, Dad. Your room is back where the guest room used to be, all duded up with its own bathroom. Do you want me to show him, Early? It looks like you have plans tonight, too."

"Yes, thank you." She lifted her chin. "I do have plans. Ben, will you be okay alone this evening?"

"Of course I—"

"No need," Nash interrupted cheerfully. "I can hang around. Even though he's probably all right by himself, I'm not comfortable with it yet."

Early thought of coming home from a date to find Nash asleep on her couch and shuddered. "I can change my plans, Nash. There's no need for you to—"

"We wouldn't hear of it, would we, Dad?" Without waiting for Ben to answer, Nash put his hands on her shoulders, turned her around, and gave her a little push. "I'll get the door if the bell rings again. Who programmed that thing anyway? I felt like yelling 'Hi-ho, Silver!' when you opened the door."

She hesitated, turning again and backing toward the hallway to her room. "Ben, are you hungry? I mean, I understand that you're no longer allowed to speak with the doctor here in the house, but you can just nod your head."

"No, we ate—"

"—on the way," Nash finished, heading toward the kitchen. "I brought him a diet list, Early. You want it posted on the fridge?"

"Sure." She grinned at Ben and said softly, "I don't know what his problem is, but we'll have a good time when he's gone."

"I'm counting on it, sugar."

The broad wink of his brown eye made her realize Nash still wore his sunglasses even though he'd been in the house for several minutes, something he never did. Concern slipped uncomfortably under her skin. "Nash?" she called.

"Go on," said Ben, shaking his head at her. "Get ready. We'll be fine."

In her room, her hair still wrapped in a towel, with mascara coating one set of eyelashes, Early thought irritably of Nash's nonstop talk, the sunglasses, his uncharacteristic appearance at her door without calling first. Good grief, he was acting like—

Oh, Nash.

She pulled her robe back on and went into the hall. "Nash?"

He appeared a moment later, his sunglasses replaced by regular ones. His eyes were darker than ever, red-rimmed, looking as smudged as though he'd rubbed them with the Irishman's proverbial sooty fingers. Had it been another man, she'd have thought he was hung over. Since it was Nash, she knew better.

"Who was it?" she asked quietly.

"I'm just tired. You know how the days off are—someone always goes into labor or needs stitches or..." His voice didn't so much stop as wind down into exhausted silence.

"Who was it?" she repeated, her hand reaching of its own volition—she couldn't have stopped it if her life depended on it—to rest on his cheek, to feel the end-of-day bristle that felt ridiculously like a caress on her fingers.

"The little Gaddis boy."

"Oh, Nash." She said it aloud this time, and wrapped him close. "You can't save them all, love. You know that."

"I know." His arms came around her, tight and hard.

It was this way every time he lost a patient who died from something other than the side-effects of old age, even worse when, like now, the loss was of a child. "The practice of family medicine is a mistake for you," a medical school professor had told him. "You can't separate the disease from the patient and just treat the disease. And it will kill you, Nash. It will kill you."

For the twenty-plus years her husband had been in practice, Early had feared his professor was right. Now that Nash was her ex-husband, she feared it even more, because she wasn't there to come home to, to listen, to hold him against his grief.

"How are his parents?" she asked. Long experience had taught her to keep him engaged in conversation. If he was talking, he couldn't retreat into a cold and angry silence where he blamed himself through the long night until daylight sent him back to work.

"Like you'd expect. They're destroyed. They—" He drew in a shuddering breath and his arms tightened spasmodically. "They thanked me for all I'd done, for trying so hard. Their baby's lying there dead with a teddy bear in the crook of his arm and they *thanked* me."

"They let him go, Nash. They knew all his life they would have to, and they did. Now you have to, too."

"I know," he said again. "I know."

She didn't know how long they stood there. Until he felt less sweaty in her arms, maybe, or until the doorframe began to hurt her back and she made some sort of sound. They parted with whispers.

"Okay?"

"Yeah, okay."

And whatever it was that made her rub her nose against his and step away and made him kiss her cheek and turn toward the living room, Early was sorry for it.

When the phone rang, she answered absently.

"I'm sorry, Mama," said Jessie. "I know you're mad because I sent him down early, but he needed you."

"It's all right, Jess." Early sighed. It wasn't really all right, not by a long shot, but how was she going to tell her daughter that?

"Are you still going on your date?"

"Yes." Although the truth was, she didn't want to. She wanted to stay here in her bathrobe and eat homemade pizza with the man who didn't want her anymore and his father. She wanted to talk to them about her half-made plans for a quilt shop, play board games, and take a walk down to the creek in the dark with Nash's arm bumping against hers.

If this was the other side, it wasn't working out very well. She didn't know how Reginald had done it.

~

"I SWEAR THIS WASN'T MY INTENTION." JOSH WALDEN LOOKED around the busy interior of McDonald's. "It just never occurred to me to make reservations. This is the Ridge, for heaven's sake."

Early swallowed a bite of her Big Mac. "Friday nights are busy everywhere you go and having Ponderosa closed down for remodeling definitely narrows our choices. Besides, this is good and the Little Theatre was terrific. When I was helping Mary Brad rehearse her lines, I had no idea she'd be such a good Mame. Of course, what can you expect from a paralegal who raises registered chickens?"

He grinned at her. "And I had no idea when Nash answered your door that I'd have such a nice evening with his wife."

Early felt the heat rise in her cheeks. "You almost didn't," she admitted. "I'm not at all comfortable with whatever my new identity is yet. It feels completely strange having your ex-husband tell you to have a good time when you leave with another man."

It wasn't yet midnight when Josh walked her to her front door, her hand clasped in his. Under the porch light, he smiled down at her. "It was fun."

"Yes."

"It was fun," he said again, "and I'd like to see you again, but you're still Nash's wife to me." He stroked a finger down the side of her face. "And to you, I think." He kissed her cheek, the touch brief but warm. "When you're ready, call me."

She nodded. "But I don't know when." She met his gaze again. She owed him that. "Or if. Don't wait."

"That's fair." He reached to open the door. "Goodnight, Early."

"SO WHAT ARE YOU GOING TO DO, JUST LET HER GO?"

Leaning on the back porch rail, Nash looked over at where his father stood at the French doors of the suite Early had prepared for him. Ben looked tired and gray in the moonlight, and Nash felt a niggle of fear. "Did you take your medicine?"

"Yes. Did you?"

"Yes."

"Are you going to answer my question?"

"Probably not."

"There are worse things than being married to your best friend."

Yeah, like not being married to her. Nash pushed the thought back. This was what he'd wanted, wasn't it? Freedom, choices, everything he'd given up when he was eighteen.

Everything Early had given up, too, though she'd never seemed to feel the regrets that had eaten away at him until they manifested themselves into a divorce.

Or had she regretted things, too? He thought of that awkward moment when he'd opened her door to Josh Walden. "Come in," he'd said. "Early's almost ready."

And then she'd come down the hall. The peach-colored sweater she wore made her lightly tanned skin glow. She had on more makeup than usual, and her hair was shorter, lighter, and brighter than it had been when she left Lexington.

He'd wanted to tell her not to go. *Stay here. We'll make pizza and talk to Dad and walk through the woods to the creek and listen to the water. You love walking. Then we'll come back and just be us.*

But he just said, "Have a good time," like he was her father or something, sketched a wave in Josh's direction, and closed the door behind them.

"Goodnight, son."

Ben's words brought him abruptly back to the present. "'Night, Dad."

When the French doors closed, Nash went to sit on a chaise. Heaviness bore down in his chest, and he prayed that it was only loneliness and upset that weighed so much. He thought of little Eric Gaddis, lying peacefully with his bear cuddled in his arm.

Dying wouldn't be so bad, he guessed.

There were definitely days when it would be easier than living.

CHAPTER 5

"Want to walk?" Early invited when she returned from her date.

Nash was pleased to notice she hadn't stayed out late, but he wasn't going to examine why it made him happy.

He set down the remote control and pushed himself to his feet. Early walked every day no matter where she was. She used to ask him to go with her, but he'd usually found reasons not to. After his angioplasty, she forced the issue and he went along, treading Canterbury Crossing's pseudo-cobblestones for the prescribed time. He'd responded to her attempts at conversation in monosyllables until she gave up and they did their three miles in a heavy silence that seemed to seep into and take over the rest of their marriage. Sometimes he'd noticed her lips moving and knew she was praying.

He wished he'd have prayed with her, but he hadn't. He wished he'd talked to her more, but the hadn't.

He wished a lot of things.

He hadn't walked since he'd moved out of the house, though he went to the rehabilitation unit at the hospital and did a stint on the treadmill three times a week.

"Where do you go?" he asked, pushing his feet into his shoes.

"I cleared a path down to the creek and keep it mowed. Mary Brad did the same thing on her side, so as long as the water's down, we walk across the rocks and go around to the road in a circle. It's about forty-five minutes. I thought it would be good for Ben—a nice break from the treadmill." She looked down at her white pants and dressy sandals. "Whoops, just a minute."

When she had donned a pair of baggy sweatpants and worn Nikes, they set out, snagging flashlights from under the kitchen sink. "No streetlights, even though the moon's out bright and big," she said, when he raised an eyebrow. "You've been out of the country too long, doctor."

"We don't have mosquitoes this big in Lexington, remember?"

"Wimp."

But she sprayed him with an evil-smelling insect repellant, and he returned the favor, covering her eyes like she was one of the grandkids, before they headed into the woods.

"I thought you walked mornings," he commented.

"I do, but I was a nervous wreck this morning."

"Something wrong?"

She shot him a look. "I haven't dated in over thirty years, Nash. Tonight was the first time and it required a lot of thought and suffering. Even more than the first time."

"More than that?" He'd been her first date, he knew, and probably her last one until tonight. Well, maybe, anyway.

"Yeah. It's harder to go on dates when you don't have a flat stomach."

"Excuse me," Nash said mildly, "but I don't remember seeing your stomach on *our* first date, or for a long time after that."

She grinned at him, the expression not making him feel any better at all. "Of course you didn't see it, but I still had to make sure it stayed flat."

As they walked farther into the woods, Early swept the beam of her flashlight across the path. "Watch out," she said, as they neared the water. "There's still some brush down here. I'm not quite done with the clearing."

And with that warning, she promptly tripped over a tree root, tossing her flashlight into the creek with a splash. Had it not been for Nash's arm hauling her against him, she would have followed the torch.

They stood, hip to hip, their gazes locked. "All we need," Nash said, "is some Cole Porter music playing."

Early gusted a sigh. "Wouldn't work even then. I don't have a swirly dress to make it convincing. I've *never* had a swirly dress."

She could see no laughter in his eyes, though, and she doubted there was any in hers. "I'm sorry," she said. "I never wore swirly dresses or pretty nightgowns. By the time I could, when I wasn't nursing babies and cleaning up after all manner of accidents, we didn't go dancing anymore anyway, and it didn't seem important, but maybe it was."

He didn't answer, just held her gaze and her hands. Irritation flickered through her. It was like one of those itches that attack inside your ear where you can't scratch.

Feeling as though she'd just discovered something about their marriage she'd rather not have known, she said, "I used to look at Joe with his glamorous wives and think how lucky we were that we didn't need the trappings. But you did, didn't you? That's why we built the house in Canterbury Crossing and the new professional building and you got upset when Jessie started seeing Noah Walden, isn't it?"

"I probably did need them," he admitted.

Her irritation deepened to anger, and she looked away from him. "You should have said so," she charged sulkily. "I wouldn't have liked it, but it would have stopped me from going on thinking everything would be all right."

He lifted a hand to turn her face back toward his. "Did you miss it?"

"Miss what?" Him touching her? She missed it every day of her life.

"Dancing."

"Well, of course, I did. Didn't—"

"You never said."

Never one to do things halfway, Early leaped into the trap. "You should have known."

"Right."

She pulled away and stepped across the creek, praying her feet didn't slip off the rocks.

You should have known.

She should have known, too, but she hadn't. She'd been too busy raising kids and congratulating herself on the success story of their lives to realize they weren't successful at all. Not really.

He didn't follow her immediately, and for a moment they stared at each other across the shallow width of water. It was like their marriage, Early thought. The differences between them were as small and clear and easily bridged as Little Cat Creek. But just as no one had ever cared enough to build a bridge over the creek, neither she nor Nash had cared enough or understood enough to repair their own connection.

"You need a bridge."

His words, so closely echoing her thoughts, startled her. "Yes." She tore her gaze away from his to look down at the water. "But it's probably too late."

NASH DIDN'T KNOW WHEN THE DAYS HAD BECOME ENDLESS. Until recently, they had never been long enough, and now here he was sitting behind his desk thinking five o'clock would never come. He wasn't sure when he'd started leaving work on time, either.

"How about dinner Saturday night? I make a mean lasagna, if I do say so who shouldn't."

He looked at Sophie Donato. She leaned against the doorframe of his office, her lab coat open over a tight little sweater. The top was deep red, with some sparkly things running through it.

A med school friend of Nash's partner, Sophie was covering Jason's practice for the summer while Jason took his entire family to Europe. She was a good doctor, a nice woman who went to church on Sundays and read to the kids in the pediatric wing when she had extra time. She was also—though Nash figured no one had used the term since about 1950—on the make.

"Come on," she cajoled. "You gotta get your feet wet sometime."

He bristled at the thought of greeting Josh Walden when he came to pick up Early. Is that what Early was doing, getting her feet wet? "Great," he said. "Where do you live?"

"The floor below yours." Sophie's smile was triumphant, and the expression made him uncomfortable. "Three doors down from your brother, a floor above your son. Does your family own the building by any chance?"

"Not yet, but I think my daughter would like to retire by the time she's thirty, so she might be buying it." Thinking of Jessie made him smile, but Sophie's answering beam told him she'd misunderstood his expression. "Seven on Saturday?"

"Yes."

He wanted her to leave. That was one reason they had comfortable private offices in the building, so that if one of them didn't feel like talking to anyone, he could go into his own inner sanctum with his name on the door and be assured of privacy.

"See you then." He looked down at the file folder on his desk, hoping she recognized the action as a dismissal.

"Bye."

The headache that had been teasing all day suddenly hit with the force of a blow, accompanied by a vague pain in his arm that disturbed Nash even more than his pounding head.

He leaned back into the creaky leather of his chair. Early's picture laughed up at him from the place it had held on his desk ever since he'd had one. Longing for her was sharp and fierce, inserting itself right in there with the headache and the pain in his arm. Maybe he could just drive down into the country and tell her it was all a mistake, that he didn't like being without her, that whatever his crisis was, they could work it out.

But they couldn't, could they?

~

"WHY AREN'T YOU DRESSED?"

Early looked down at her sweats. It was Sunday, so they even matched. "I am dressed."

Mary Brad sighed. "You can't wear sweats to church."

"I don't go to church." Hadn't in—good heavens, years, since Nash missed more Sundays than he didn't and the kids were old enough to make their own choices. She still believed, still prayed, still gave money to the church they'd attended in Lexington; she just didn't go anymore.

"Then it's time you started. You're on the Ridge now." Mary Brad looked at her watch. "There's time enough for me to drink some coffee while you get ready."

"Mary Brad, I—"

"Lou Ann's boy John David is the pastor. You know he'd be so proud to see you there."

Oh, Lou Ann. She'd been one of the four little Four Corners girls in the same grade, living directly across Little Cat. They'd been best friends all the way through childhood because there'd been no one else to be best friends with.

Lou Ann's husband, John Hendry, had been killed in the coal mines along with Mary Brad's husband Paul years ago when John David and his sisters were toddlers. When Lou Ann had died of ovarian cancer a couple of years ago, Nash had worried because for the first time in all the years they'd been together, Early couldn't stop crying.

Lou Ann would come to church in a heartbeat if one of Early's sons was preaching. She'd wear a dress and put a whopping big donation in the collection plate, then she'd tell everyone she knew that Early's youngun was a mighty fine preacher even if that particular boy couldn't string two sentences together without a stammer.

"I would have called yesterday, but I knew your girls were here." Mary Brad slipped off her heels and went to the kitchen, calling over her shoulder. "Word will get over to your mama that you came to church at the Corners, and she'll be fit to be tied that she can't grieve for your lost soul anymore."

"Doesn't Mama still go to church there?"

"Oh, mercy, no. She goes in Pleasant Hill now." Mary Brad grinned at her, leaning around the doorjamb. "They look down on us over at Four Corners, on account of we didn't join the Ridge Coalition of Churches, and we've never paved our parking lot."

"Well, shame on you."

When Early came into the kitchen dressed in a skirt and loose cardigan, Ben was at the table and Mary Brad was cooking his daily oatmeal.

"Want to go to church, Ben?" Early got his medications and put them in front of him.

"Not today, honey. I'm kind of tired."

He looked tired. She swallowed a quick jolt of panic. "I'll stay here with you." She exchanged a look with Mary Brad when the other woman brought Ben's bowl to the table.

"You most certainly will not." He glared at her, though the expression didn't frighten her any more than it ever had. "Early, there were times even before I had a heart attack that I was worn out. Remember?"

In the car with Mary Brad, Early got her cell phone out of her purse. With many long-suffering sighs, she'd finally started carrying it with her even though the reception on the Ridge was spotty at best. "Call your dad," she told Nash's sleepy voice. "He's too tired."

She hung up and turned off the phone, lightened by relief she didn't want to examine too closely. When Nash called last night concerning Ben's medication, there had been a woman's laughing voice in the background. Early didn't think she could bear it if that same voice had been there this morning.

"GOD IS GOOD!"

"All the time," Early murmured automatically, preparing to step into the fourth pew on the left behind Mary Brad. When she'd been a child, they'd sat in the sixth pew on the right, and she'd almost gone into that one out of long-ago habit, but a young woman with a baby and two toddlers had looked up in surprise and Early had drawn back with a self-conscious smile.

"Folks!" The voice was vibrant and coming her way. "I want you to look at this morning's blessing. It's Miss Early Winslow McGrath come to see us."

She looked up to where Lou Ann's blue eyes shone in a handsome young face, and then she was pulled into the minister's embrace. "Oh, Miss Early, you do make me miss my mama."

Early hugged him back. "You make me miss her, too, John

David," she said, a catch in her voice, "especially now that you've embarrassed me beyond redemption, which she would have loved."

"She would, wouldn't she?" He beamed at her, and reached past her to squeeze Mary Brad's hand. "Guess I'll have to behave, with both of you here. Only one missing is Miss Emily."

Early remembered when to stand, when to sit, when to bow her head. She remembered the words to the hymns she'd grown up with, knew to fold the bills she put into the collection plate because that was just what people did when they didn't want to appear either ostentatious or embarrassed. She knew to stand after the offering and sing, "Praise God from whom all blessings flow..." When John David called for pies and free labor for the upcoming ice cream social, she offered four pies and two hours. Spiritually and emotionally, coming to the little church on the corner had been a good thing.

"Maybe a centerpiece?" John David said. "I've heard wonderful things about your garden."

"And maybe a quilt for a silent auction," came from across the aisle of the sanctuary. "I've heard great things about your quilting, too."

Early recognized Mary Brad's father's voice and scowled at her friend. "I'm not fast enough to make one between now and Saturday, Mr. Wilkins, but I can probably have one ready for the soup supper in November. I must admit, it's fun being so popular, though. Where were you all when I was in high school?"

As they left the church, John David took both her hands. "I'm so glad you came," he said quietly. "I remember you two and Mama and Miss Emily sitting on the bank of Little Cat while we children played, only I think you all were having more fun. Having you and Miss Mary Brad here keeps me from getting too full of myself."

She laughed. "We certainly don't want that, now, do we?

When can your family come for supper? Ben would love to see you; he and your granddad were old cronies."

"No family. Just me. As Mama would tell me, over and over, I haven't found anyone to put up with me yet. But I'd love to see Ben. I knew he was back but hadn't gotten over to see him yet. So I'll come whenever you say."

"Friday," she said.

"Friday it is."

Driving home, with her cardigan in the back seat and her shoes kicked off, Early sighed contentedly. "Thanks for taking me." She smiled over at her friend. "I think I've come home."

CHAPTER 6

EVAN CONSENTED—SLEEPILY—TO TAKE HIS FATHER'S ON-CALL day, and Nash was on the road down to the Ridge ten minutes after hearing Ben's voice on the phone. It wasn't that he had sounded ill or even overly tired; he'd just sounded wrong.

Nash enjoyed the drive to the Ridge. He loved Lexington and always had, but there was something about going where all was familiar that was soothing. He didn't blame his father for wanting to come back, but he wondered if Early was regretting her decision yet.

His wife had always been busy. With the kids, with his mom, with her parents. She volunteered at the hospital, the library, the church they attended before they'd somehow stopped. She never went to college, although she earned her GED years ago, but she'd always studied. She became a master gardener, although she didn't join the garden club because she didn't feel as though she fit in. An avid quilter from the first time Emily Grosvenor's mother gave her scraps and a needle, she used to sew far into the night while he read and watched television. The den had been the one cluttered room in the Canterbury Crossing house, because widescreen televisions, shelves of medical, quilting, and gardening books, and Rosie's old quilting frame didn't lend themselves to neatness.

It had been, he realized, his favorite room in the house.

Early didn't have any of that to keep her busy on the Ridge. She hadn't been back long enough to find places to volunteer, plus Ben needed her presence on a fairly steady basis. With no society to speak of, even though Mary Brad lived just across the creek, how long would it be before Early found herself watching the clock till bedtime?

No one opened the door to his parents' old house when he rang, though the chime had changed from the "William Tell Overture" to "Amazing Grace." Frowning, he walked around the side of the house. The brick sidewalk was still wet, so Early must have watered her flowers this morning.

He came around the corner just as Ben lifted the hose to water the geraniums that sat in pots on the back porch. His father nearly drowned him.

"I'm a little old for that, Dad," he said, shaking his wet hair back from his face and taking off his glasses. He glared over at Early, who sat convulsed with laughter behind a small quilt frame. "That's why I came down, Early, to be your day's entertainment."

"And I do so appreciate it, Dr. McGrath," she said sweetly, still laughing. "Sit down. I'll get you a towel and some coffee. You want some cookies?"

"Yes, please." He pulled a chair into the sun and sat down. He dragged a dry piece of shirt around from behind him to wipe off his prescription sunglasses. "Dad? You doing all right?"

"Why does everyone keep asking me that?" Ben turned the hose to the containers of hens and chickens that edged the porch steps. "I'm fine."

"Well, you don't sound fine. You worried me and the grouchy doctor both to death today." Early came out the door with a tray. "Here, have some decaf. It'll sweeten you up." She handed him a cup, then walked over and gave Nash a mug along with a plate of cookies and the fluffy white towel that lay over the shoulder of the sleeveless yellow sweater she wore with a black skirt. Under the cookies on the plate was the paper with Ben's blood pressure recordings written in Early's neat hand.

Nash read the list as unobtrusively as possible. There was nothing attention-getting there; the numbers were on the high side of normal and consistent. Dad's color was good and he seemed to be active.

"So, why are you dressed up?" Nash asked Early. "You have a date?" Like it was his business if she did. Nevertheless, he felt hollow waiting for her to answer.

She scowled at him. "I went to church. I hope you don't have a problem with that." She returned to her chair behind the quilt rack, retrieving her reading glasses from the table at her side and taking up a needle.

He didn't want to remember the days of sitting all-in-a-row in church. It reminded him that the Lord hadn't moved—he had. "What's that you're working on?"

"A quilt for a lawyer in the office where Mary Brad works. He commissioned it for his wife. It's a wall-hanging, but outsize to hang in the multilevel entry to their house."

He scooted his chair over to look closer. "Did you design it?"

She looked up with surprise. "Not exactly. It's a log cabin pattern tweaked a bit here and there."

He thought of the huge quilt that hung on the waiting room wall of the medical building—people stopped and stared at it and walked away smiling. And the little one over the train table in the children's alcove; the parents loved it as much as the kids did. He wondered if he'd ever told her those things. Probably not.

"We need a new one for the children's area," he heard himself saying. "We have to wash that one so often it's begun to fade."

"Okay." She looked pleased, a little smile tucking itself into her cheek.

"Dad?" He drew his attention away from Early with an effort. "You want to play some chess or something?"

"No." Ben shook his head, looking off into the distance. "Tell you what I *would* like—I'd like to go to the cemetery." He smiled, but there was no joy in the expression. "There are days that I miss your mother almost more than I can stand. This is one of them."

Nash met Early's eyes over her quilting hoop. *Why didn't we think of that?*

"I don't know," she said aloud, softly, and they smiled at each other. The mind-reading, sentence-finishing parts of long marriage were things Nash missed.

Along with a lot of other things. The picture rose in his mind again of the McGraths filling a pew in church. Early and the children had attended long after Nash became a Christmas-and-Easter Christian. What had made him rearrange his priorities?

Regret was heavy sometimes.

Early rose, pushing the quilt neatly aside. "I'll get some flowers, Ben." As she went past her father-in-law, she put a hand on his arm. "You have to tell us things. We don't always catch on, and we get scared."

"I know, sugar." He squeezed her hand. "It's hard, though, depending on people." His gaze went past her to Nash. "It's not a good lesson I taught him, is it, to not need anyone?"

Nash wanted to argue, but he couldn't. In his quest to be the best family physician he could, to be the one who *was* needed, he'd forgotten to be a sharing husband, father, and child of God. He'd forgotten to share the needs he *had*.

"Would you take some for Susan's grave, too, Nash? And Lou Ann's—her boy preached today. Made me miss her." Early got clippers from the garden shed and moved quickly around the flower beds.

"Why don't you come along?" he asked.

"All right." She handed him the clippers. "Here. Get some more zinnias and daisies for Lou Ann's grave. She loved bright colors."

"She did, didn't she? Used to wear those swirly skirts, like Mexican women did in movies, whether they were in style or not."

They laughed. Another shared memory.

"I'm going up to change." Early fled.

SUSAN'S GRAVE SAT AT THE BACK OF THE CEMETERY IN A SPOT BY itself, something Early had never quite forgiven her parents for. They could have bought an additional lot in the family plot nearer the front, but they hadn't. They'd buried her in shame back by the building where the lawnmowers were kept.

When Nash began making money (and Early stopped working at McDonald's), they came down one weekend and bought the lots that surrounded Susan's and planted a blue spruce and perennial flowers on them. Then they put a white picket fence around the whole plot and Nash hung a sign on the gate proclaiming it to be "Susan's Garden."

There were always fresh flowers on the grave, even when family members hadn't been there for a while. On this visit, a shepherd's hook was pushed into the ground beside the marker, a musical chime dancing from the curved metal in the light wind.

They made a desultory stop at Early's father's grave, leaving flowers and standing silently for a moment before going on, taking the long way around the pretty little cemetery to give Ben some time with Rosie.

"I hate what you've done to us." Early's gaze rested on where her father-in-law knelt, but her words were for Nash alone. "Most of the time, I'm so mad at you I don't know whether to spit or chew nails, but I'm still grateful you're alive, Nash McGrath, glad you're my children's father, so please do take care of yourself."

He looked startled. "Where did that come from?"

She sighed. "I don't know. Seeing Lou Ann's boy this morning, maybe, then coming here. John and Mary Brad's husband Paul both dying in the mine like that. Lou Ann being so young when she left us—her kids were just barely grown up. Life's so short, and we mess it up every time we turn around." She sighed again, deeper this time, looking away from him to where the cottonwoods that rimmed the cemetery whispered with the wind. "I just don't know."

She walked ahead, leaving him to do whatever he wanted. It was so strange, being divorced but still somehow connected. Life couldn't go on; it just sat there rocking back and forth like a hobby horse.

Who was the woman whose laughter she'd heard over the phone?

"You were right about the divorce," she said abruptly, when he caught up with her. Her eyes and her hands both felt hot and dry, and she couldn't find anything to do with either of them. She jabbed her hands into the pockets of her shorts and looked away from him, trying to find a spot that didn't hurt. Her voice, surprisingly enough, was steady. "It was time. If we're not going to have a life together, it's time to have one apart. I couldn't see it then, when you insisted we file, but you were right."

"But I—" He sounded perplexed, and faintly alarmed. He stopped, putting a hand on her arm and waiting till she glanced up at him. "Is this because of Josh?"

"Who?" She stared at him, befuddled. "Oh, Josh. No. No. It's...I don't know how to—" She straightened her shoulders and met his gaze head on. "It's because it's time to get to the other side."

CHAPTER 7

"EARLINE WINSLOW MCGRATH, YOU'RE GOING TO REGRET THIS ridiculous divorce, you mark my words." Francie glared at her daughter over the top of the ladder Early was standing on to wash Francie's windows.

"Hand me the Windex, will you, Mother? I dropped it."

"What am I supposed to tell people?"

"What people?" Early took the bottle and sprayed the glass. And rubbed, clenching her hand tight around the soft cloth.

"People at church, at the garden club, the home economics club and down at Waylon's—Patty's always talking about you. If I have to hear one more time about how Evan was almost born in the produce section, I'm going to smack her one. She's there to sell groceries, not embarrass me to death."

"Embarrass you how?" asked Early. "I hardly ever drop eggs in the aisle anymore, especially since I buy them from Mary Brad, and Patty's been a great friend to us over the years."

"You'd only been married for six months, for goodness sake."

"Seven, and it was thirty years ago. I'm sorry if you're still embarrassed by that."

"And now you've divorced Nash over some harebrained

notion that you don't love each other anymore. Love, schmove. Handsome husbands with six-figure incomes who are nice men in the bargain don't grow on trees, especially when you're over forty."

"Well, then, I'll know not to be checking in trees when I'm on the lookout for another man." The idea of looking for a man tickled her somehow, and she had to turn her back to snicker into Francie's cobweb-free corner.

"It's not funny. You won't like it when you're alone over there in the holler with no one to talk to."

"Is Ben going somewhere I don't know about?"

"He's had one heart attack. It can't be that long before another one follows. Him and me, we're at that falling-apart age. I hope you made sure he's leaving that house to you, since you gave up the beautiful place there in Lexington to come take care of him."

"I bought it from him," Early said. "I wanted something of my own. If I'm going to live without Nash, I needed it to be somewhere separate from where I lived with him. And don't tell me—" She held up a forestalling hand. "I know he grew up there, but the house is entirely different from what it was then." She was being less than honest; much of what the house meant to her had to do with the memories it held. The shelves Ben built in the window above the sink for Rosie's collection of salt-and-pepper shakers, the doorway into the pantry where the children's heights were marked from toddler-size to the over-six-feet Evan and Logan became.

"Well, that's just plain foolish," Francie snorted.

Early looked around the painfully neat kitchen of her mother's house. "Look around here, Mother. There's not a sign anywhere that you were ever married to Dad. No pictures, no old chair that was his, nothing."

"I was married to your father for over thirty years. I'm not likely to forget him," said Francie stiffly.

There was something in her voice Early had never heard before, or maybe she'd never listened—that sometimes seemed to be a pattern for her. "Mama?" she said quietly. She looked down at where her mother stood at the refrigerator door, surprised by her absolute stillness. "Mama?" she said again.

Francie blinked rapidly and turned away, keeping her arthritic balance by grasping the edge of the countertop. "If you're through with the windows, Earline, I'd appreciate it if you'd scrub out the bathtub. I just can't get down there anymore like I used to."

Whatever the moment had been, it was over. Early stifled a sigh. Cleaning bathtubs wasn't high on her list of fun things to do, either.

It was right up there with getting divorced from a man you had a sneaking suspicion you still loved.

"MAMA, WHO DO YOU THINK HE WAS? DO YOU THINK HE KNEW about me?"

Sarah had asked the question before, several times over the years, but never on the Ridge, holding an armful of daisies destined for her mother's grave. The trek to the cemetery was becoming very familiar.

"I think he didn't know, honey." Early put away the gardening tools. "Your mother didn't know, either, I don't think. None of us were especially knowledgeable in those days." She grinned at Sarah. "That's how your brother came to almost be born in Waylon's."

"I know, and I love Daddy. I surely wouldn't want another father. But there's a part of me that still wonders, you know? What If I get married someday and have a baby who looks like someone on the Ridge? What if I marry someone from down here and find out he's my brother?" Sarah shuddered. "Evan and

Logan are brothers enough for anybody. I don't need any more of them, either."

Early laughed. "Come on, darlin'—let's go. You want to ride bikes? It's only a couple of miles and a beautiful day. I have a basket on my bike for the flowers."

"Sure." Sarah followed her to the garage. "When did you start riding a bicycle?"

"When I was at an auction with Josh and they were selling six of them in a batch. I bought them and sold two of them to Josh for half the money I'd paid. Seemed like a good deal to me. This way, anyone who comes down can ride."

"So." Sarah pushed two bicycles out and swung a long, slender leg over the back of one. "You're still seeing Mr. Walden?"

"Some. We're friends." Early closed the garage door and mounted her bike, stopping to straighten the flowers in the basket. "I'm sorry. I know it's hard on you kids."

"It is. You and Daddy are still a unit to us."

They rode slowly toward the cemetery, enjoying the fresh morning air.

"Mama?"

"Uh-huh." Although, true to the old saying, one didn't forget how to ride a bike, long years away from it did tend to make a person both slow and clumsy. Early had to concentrate.

"I need to tell you something."

There was enough hesitancy in Sarah's voice to send dread shivering down Early's spine, giving her gooseflesh even on the warm and humid day. "Uh-huh?" she said again, standing on wobbly legs to ride up a long hill.

"Jessie and I talked about it and decided you should know even if Daddy didn't tell you. The boys," she added offhandedly, "thought we should mind our own business."

"Oh." She crested the hill and sat down again, breathing hard, her legs weak and bumping against the frame of the bike. "Go on."

"He's seeing someone, too."

Early would have thought, since she'd ridden so little and was just getting her bicycle legs, that the world was already moving in an unhurried manner, but she was amazed by how much time slowed with her daughter's words.

"Oh?" Her lips felt stiff and her voice sounded high.

Don't ask who. Be nonchalant. It's none of your business, not anymore, even though you've already heard her laugh and hated her for it.

"Who's he seeing?" She spoke over her loud inner voice, deliberately lowering her outer one and sounding a great deal like a frog.

"That doctor who's taking Jason's place for the summer."

"Sophie?"

Sophie was beautiful, with long, slim hands and flashing Italian eyes. She was at least three inches taller than Early and, even though she carried a few extra pounds, she carried them in better places than Early. She dressed well, the texture of her clothes making you want to reach out and rub the fabric between your fingers. Jeans and cotton sweaters just didn't hold up in the comparison.

It was one thing to sort-of-date Josh Walden, who knew where her heart lay and made no demands on her emotions. It was quite another to think of Nash with someone else. And not just any someone, but one with a name and a face and long legs.

This wasn't like riding a bicycle, not at all. It was definitely more like the Ferris wheel, and she was feeling mildly nauseated right along with it.

"Oh," she said. "Well." She hopped off inside the cemetery entrance. It took her three pushes to get the kickstand in place and three deep breaths before she was certain she wasn't going to throw up.

While Sarah fussed over the flowers in Susan's Garden, Early carried an arrangement to where Rosie was buried. She sat beside the grave, groaning a little when she bent her knees. "What do I do now, Rosie? Where do I go from here?" she whispered. "I know I'm in the right place. I do. This is where God wants me to be, but I don't know what's next. I'm not sure I've got the listening to Him down pat."

It would be, she realized, a life completely of her own. Her children were adults, Ben grew stronger with each passing day, and Nash was no longer the other half of her own personal equation.

This, then, was the other side she'd been so cavalier about reaching. Was this how Reginald the rooster felt, as though he'd likely died, but his body had forgotten to fall down? *Help me up, Lord, please. With You, I can do anything. Without You, I can do nothing.*

"Hey, Miss Early."

The voice seemed to come from far away, and she stared for a disjointed second at Rosie's marker before looking up. "Oh," she said. "John David. Hello."

He stretched a hand to help her to stand. "Are you all right?" His handsome features creased in concern. "You look pale."

"No, I'm fine." She tried smiling, surprised her mouth still worked, still stretched into the proper shape to keep people from worrying, but saw that John David's attention was elsewhere, seemingly focused on Sarah's coppery head in Susan's Garden.

Oh. Oh, Lou Ann, can you imagine?

"You haven't talked to my daughter since you were both in Little League, have you?" she said, and raised her voice slightly. "Sarah?"

Somehow it came as no surprise that neither of the younger people paid the slightest bit of attention to her after that.

"I'm going now," she said finally, after she'd rearranged the flowers on Rosie's grave—again, "and my legs are plumb worn out from pedaling. I'd rather walk home. John David, would you want to ride my bike to my house? There are hamburgers grilled outside in it for you."

"I'd be happy to, Miss Early." He flashed his mother's smile, and Early felt a wave of nostalgia for the friend she missed.

Ben was on the porch when she got home, looking anxious, and her car was out of the garage and pointed toward the road. She reached for her phone, wondering if she'd missed its ring, and realized she hadn't taken it with her.

"Ben?" She hurried to where he stood, and his arm came around her.

"It's Francie, honey. She's fallen. You need to get to the hospital. Your purse is already in the car with your phone in it." He shook his head to forestall questions. "That's all I know. They called not ten minutes ago. Do you want me to go with you?"

"No." She kissed his cheek. "Stay near the phone, okay?"

On the somewhat-over-the-speed-limit drive to Pleasant Hill, Early prayed for her mother.

And for herself. She could feel the trap closing.

"It's just a blessing it wasn't my hip is all," said Francie fretfully. "Seems whenever someone breaks their hip it's the end to everything. There's worse things than a broken ankle and a couple of cracked ribs."

"Much worse," Early said. "What on earth were you doing on the stepstool, Mother? I had just cleaned the tops of the cupboards."

"There was a cobweb up there—you know how they sneak in overnight—and it seemed easier to get up there and whip at it with a towel than go clear to the laundry room for the broom. The Lord punishes laziness, that's for sure." She looked at her daughter with a jaundiced eye. "Land sakes, Earline, your hands are filthy, and what on earth are you doing out in public in those clothes?"

Early looked down at her faded denim shorts and equally faded green tank top. "I was doing flowers and riding a bicycle. Neither thing called for me to be either clean or neat," she said mildly.

Francie reached up to try to straighten the hair around her face. "I should talk." Her voice was both faint and fretful. "I must look a mess."

Pity surged inside of Early, in the place that love for her mother belonged, and she reached for Francie's purse. "Do you have a comb in here?"

"In the side pocket."

Also in the zippered pocket were two laminated snapshots. One was of Early and Susan, dressed in ruffled swimsuits and laughing uproariously for the camera. They'd probably been eight and five, and even then Susan's beauty had been startling in its purity. The other was of a handsome man who looked familiar but Early couldn't identify. She squinted at the photograph for a moment, and opened her mouth to as who it was. Was there a black-sheep uncle hanging somewhere on Francie's secret family tree?

But then she looked at her mother, felt pity again, and didn't ask, just combed Francie's permed hair as neatly as she could and handed her the lipstick complete-with-mirror that had been with the comb. "You better do this. If I put it on, you'll look like a clown."

The doctor, who looked no older than Evan and whose blue

jeans made her think of Nash, came in shortly. "I think maybe an overnight stay, Ms. Winslow. What do you think?" he said cheerily. "Your doctor's away for the weekend—camping out on Big Cat and fishing with his grandkids—and I'd feel better if you got some real rest. We'll immobilize that ankle for you and then get you to a room with a view. You'll have to get it casted in a few days. That work all right for you?"

"Oh." Francie looked frightened. "I'd really rather go home."

"You just rest a minute," he said. "I'll talk to your daughter in the hall—we doctors have to have our secrets, you know."

Nash was striding down the hall when they stepped outside the door, and Early felt relief slide like warm liquid through her bones.

He didn't speak to Early, just said, "Dr. Michaels?" and accepted the proffered chart. "We're going to the family waiting room for a bit," he told the other doctor. "I'll be able to catch up with you in the ER? Francie's comfortable?"

"You bet." Dr. Michaels named an unpronounceable medication—presumably what had been in the hypodermic a nurse had emptied into Francie's hip—and Nash nodded approval before putting a hand at the back of Early's waist to urge her ahead of him down the hall.

In the deserted room with its muted mauve furniture and out-of-date magazines, the attendant pointed at the coffee, said, "Fresh," and left them to their privacy, closing the door behind her.

"What does it say?" asked Early, handing Nash a cup and sitting in a chair at right angles from his. Their knees bumped, and she stopped her hand in midair when she reached to pat his leg as she would have in days gone by.

"It's a bad break," he said, either not noticing or pretending not to, "and she's going to have considerable pain from those ribs. She's not going to heal fast." He was frowning at the chart in front of him. "Her blood pressure's worse than Dad's was before his heart attack, and she's on cholesterol-lowering medicine. Did you know that?"

"No." Early rolled her eyes. "My goodness, what a wonderful health profile we're passing down to our kids."

Nash ignored her. "No sign of diabetes. That's a good thing. She needs to spend the night here, though. She's shocky. And then she needs a week or so in interim care."

"She'll be okay at my house, won't she?"

"No. You can't pick her up if she needs to be lifted, for one thing, and for another, I want to keep her on a morphine pump for a few days. But she's going to need a place to go home to, Early, and you'd be better off spending the time either getting a room in your house ready for her or finding someone to stay with her at hers. It's not going to be a short-term thing." He hesitated. "Dad can come back to Lexington with me for a while and she can have his rooms."

"No, Nash, he can't." She didn't mean for it to, but her voice rose. Anger and fear threaded through it like melting sugar in pulled taffy. "You can't keep steamrollering people's lives to suit your own wants."

"Oh, come on, Early," he snapped. "We can do without histrionics."

She leaned toward him. "This isn't melodrama—this is the real deal. You can't push your father around when and where it suits you. He's a grown man with a mind of his own, and he doesn't want to stay in your apartment in Lexington. If you don't believe me, you can ask him. And what he says goes."

"He would want to make things as easy for you as possible," he argued.

"We're not talking about easier for me or you either one. We're talking about your father and my mother." She met his glare with one of her own. "We're not pushing them around, and if you want to add custody of them to my responsibility in the divorce decree, go ahead. That would be nice for you: get rid of your boring wife, your sick father, and your difficult mother-in-law in one fell swoop."

He sighed. "Could we please have just one conversation in which you don't mention that I'm the reason we're divorced? Contrary to what you may believe, that is not the only event of importance in our lives either together or apart. There are other things that matter, our parents included."

She opened her mouth, then closed it again. Did she do that? Really, did she? It was all well and good to make Nash feel guilty now and then—she rather hoped she did—but she didn't intend to make a life's work of being a victim. She was woman, hear her roar.

"I'm sorry," she said quietly. "You're right, of course."

She got up, moving to stand at the window. It was dusk, and the lights in the hospital parking lot were coming on. Where had the afternoon gone? She sipped her lukewarm coffee and closed her eyes.

She was so tired.

"Early."

She didn't answer, couldn't, just shook her head.

"Early," he said again, from behind her.

He took her cup from her and pulled her close, cozying her head into the spot on his shoulder where it fit so well, and all the roar went right out of her.

"You know," she said, her voice muffled against the cotton knit of his polo shirt, "I feel so guilty because I don't *want* to take care of Mother. I've never felt that way with Ben, not once."

"Mothers and daughters, I've heard, have complicated relationships." A smile slipped into his voice. "Why, Jessica Darcy and Sarah have often mentioned to me that they're already looking into putting you into the home. Looking ahead, you know, to when you get *really* difficult."

She couldn't help it, she laughed, and lifted her head. "Thank you, Dr. McGrath."

He stroked a gentle finger down her cheek. "It'll be okay," he promised.

And just as she had for over thirty years, Early believed him.

CHAPTER 8

"You can't give up everything." Jessie stood with her arms spread across the doorway to what had once been an enclosed porch off the kitchen and was now Early's sewing room. "Grandpa has the new master suite downstairs, which is fine, and you've furnished the whole place with the eventuality of a wheelchair in mind, which is also fine. But this room is yours, Mama, and you're not giving it up."

"Sweetheart, I really do appreciate your protective instincts." Early tried to step around her. "But what do you suggest I do with your grandmother? The garden shed, no matter what your brothers suggest, is out, and the building Noah's putting up for the quilt shop isn't done enough."

"That's why we're down here this weekend, Mom." Evan came into the kitchen with a nephew on his shoulders. "We're going to make the dining room—which you don't use anyway—into a temporary guest room. Noah just got here complete with tools."

"Noah?" A riot of color came, went, and came again in Jessie's face.

"Hi, Jess." Noah, with Anna and Logan's younger son under

his arm, stepped around Evan. "Hey, Miss Early. You all right with this?"

Early looked around at her children. She'd raised them; she guessed she might as well trust them.

"Yeah," she said, "I'm okay."

Two hours later, when Noah and Jessie were standing toe-to-toe and shouting and Evan and Logan were two rooms apart and shouting, she wasn't sure. "They've certainly gotten louder since they grew up," she mentioned to Anna, as they sat on the back porch stringing green beans. "This is what you have to look forward to."

Anna grinned at her. "You love it, too, don't you?"

"Sure do," Early said cheerfully, and raised her voice. "Evan? Logan? If you're going to fight, take it outside."

They thumped onto the porch a minute later, still yelling, interior doors slamming behind them. Logan stopped to kiss Anna and Evan followed suit.

"Get your own wife." Logan pushed him.

"But I like yours," Evan whined, and then they were laughing and able to go back inside.

Early and Anna had just resumed stringing beans when Noah came past them. "I have to go outside for a minute," he said succinctly, "because I really want to cuss and the preacher's in there. Your daughter," he added, just before the door swung shut behind him, "is unreasonable and a complete pain in the neck."

"I know." Early spoke into the ensuing silence, waiting.

It didn't take long. Jessie threw herself onto the porch. "Mother!"

There were reasons for living fifty-seven miles away from your children. Early narrowed her gaze on her daughter. "Stop it."

"Well, tell him—"

"Jessica Darcy, he's thirty years old, and I didn't raise him. I'm not telling him anything, and if *you* want to tell him something, go outside. Just remember that you are a lawyer, not a carpenter, so you do not want to embarrass yourself by telling him how to do his job."

Jessie's mouth opened, then closed. "You have a point," she conceded stiffly, and knelt to string a handful of beans. "Are we having these for supper?"

"These are for tomorrow. Pizza for supper."

"Miss Early." Noah came back onto the porch from the yard, his cheeks still flushed. "What do you think of punching a hole in the wall between the dining room and the half bath beside the laundry room? If we replace the big vanity with a small one and reduce the size of the closet, there'd be room for a handicap-accessible shower in there."

Something inside Early screamed, "No!" She knew, in her head, that Francie might never go home. Facing that possibility with the permanency of a handicap-accessible bathroom horrified her.

Aloud, she said quietly, "It's probably a good idea."

"It was Jess's," Noah admitted, his green gaze sweeping past her to meet Jessie's brown one.

The crew worked until five o'clock, stopping when Nash pulled into the driveway in a rental truck with a freestanding shower unit strapped in its bed. He left it for the boys to unload and found Early in the kitchen.

"Why are you doing this?" he said without preamble, going to the coffeepot. "You're going to turn this into a nursing home with yourself as an administrator if you're not careful."

"I do believe," she said, spreading pizza sauce over a thin crust, "you were the one who mentioned just a week ago that Mother would need to stay with me or have fulltime care at home. She couldn't afford that for long."

"You know I'll help."

"She's my responsibility."

"Move over." Nash turned to stand beside her, reaching for a bowl of chopped onion and green and red pepper. His arm tangled with hers, and for a moment they stood and looked at each other, their bare skin warm where it touched. "Funny," he said. "I still want to be with you."

She smiled, though it shook around the edges. "I'm not sure, but I think I'm glad about that."

He pulled his gaze away from hers and sprinkled the vegetables on the pizzas.

She followed with cheese, three kinds freshly grated and mixed together the way they liked it, and thought making pizza with Josh Walden probably wouldn't be the same, either. He wouldn't know how.

There were other things about making pizza, too. They'd made it the night Logan and Anna came home from college in the middle of the week and told them they were pregnant and dropping out of school to marry. When her cold and taciturn father had passed away, Early made three batches of dough for pizza crust and hated herself because she was unable to grieve. The night Nash told her he was leaving, they'd made pizza together as they did now, their movements quick and seamless even as all the stitched-together parts of their marriage ripped wide asunder.

"I hear"—the words came hard and hurtful—"you're seeing Sophie."

He hesitated. "Yes."

"I need to know," she said quietly, "if there was someone else while we were still together."

She hadn't asked that before, had almost convinced herself it didn't matter. But, even now that the divorce was final, she found that it did matter. It did.

"No." He slid the pizzas into the oven, his back to her. "And there were some times I wished there *were* someone else for one of us. At least then there would have been some kind of tangible reason we were so unhappy together."

She stared at him, waiting for him to turn and face her. "I wasn't unhappy."

"I've known you for forty years and lived with you for thirty, Early McGrath. Believe me when I say I know when you're happy and when you're not, and whether you want to admit it or not, you were as miserable as I was."

"You're wrong," she said, going past him to the coffeepot and pouring for them both.

"No." He took a cup from her, their fingers touching and curving around each other the way hands do when their owners have been connected forever and ever. "I'm not."

"I don't like to put you out, Earline," said Francie fretfully, picking at the squares on the quilt that covered her legs where she sat on the back porch. "There's times I think maybe shooting people when they get to be useless would be a good idea."

"You're not putting me out, Mother." Early handed her a colander of potatoes. "Here, peel. Ben takes half the skin away when he does it."

"I heard that," came from the path that led from the front of the house. "You don't pay well enough to complain, young lady."

She laughed. "You know calling me 'young lady' will save you every time."

Ben came around the corner and stepped onto the porch, tossing part of the mail onto the table beside Early's chair and carrying the rest over to where Francie sat. "It's perishingly hot today," he said. "I recall how Rosie wanted air conditioning for years before I gave in and had it installed. Then I liked it so well I used to pretend it was all my idea."

"I remember that." Early smiled at him. "And then Rosie would pretend to get mad at you." She moved toward where the small quilt frame sat, stopping when she saw Francie's expression. "Mother? You all right?"

"We didn't have air conditioning, either," her mother said, as though Early hadn't spoken. "He"—that's what she almost always called Early's father, never "Earl" or even "Dad"—"wouldn't hear of it. Said we couldn't afford it. He'd never spend a dime if a nickel would do on me or you girls, either."

By the time she got her mom into bed that night and gave Ben his medication and talked him into going to bed, too, Early was exhausted. When she finally sat down without the prospect of jumping up in the next two minutes, her tired legs throbbed from toes to thigh.

"I'm not sure I can do this," she told Mary Brad over a glass of sweet tea.

Her friend gave her a bracing smile. "You can."

"Does your dad ever talk about my folks?" asked Early.

Mary Brad considered, staring off into the woods. "He and your dad had a falling-out at some point. And he only asks about your mama in passing. Why?"

"I don't know. I think this fall has got Mother thinking about her own mortality or something, and she's saying things about my father she'd never in a million years have said before. And I found a picture in her purse of a man I don't know though I'm sure I've seen him somewhere. She knew I saw it, too, and she never said a word about it. That's not like her. Good grief, if she could figure out a way to make my own life not any of my business, she would; she's sure not going to share part of hers."

"You know," said Mary Brad, refilling their glasses, "she could probably run your life a lot better than you do."

"Speaking of minding our own business, have you heard from Joe?"

"We talk." And then Mary Brad clammed up and wouldn't say another word.

"That's crummy. You know all my dating woes. You always have."

"Right. You've dated two men in your entire life, and neither one of them ever created much in the way of woes," scoffed Mary Brad. "About your mom, though, I think you're just going to have to bite the bullet and ask her. The most she can do is disown you, and let's face it, she's done that before and you survived."

The next afternoon, Early poured decaf for her mother and stepped in where angels would fear to tread, pretty sure she could taste gunpowder in her mouth. "Did you ever love anyone besides Dad?" She twirled the ostrich feather duster around the salt and pepper shakers Ben had unearthed from his belongings and studiously avoided her mother's eyes.

"I'd say love's overrated, wouldn't you?" said Francie caustically. "Judging by you and Nash, anyway."

"I'll always love Nash whether we're married or not, and I can't be sorry for it, either." She picked up the purple cow saltshaker the girls had given Rosie for a birthday. "What's the matter? Don't want to answer my question?"

"Not particularly." The older woman sighed. "I'm not proud of everything I've done in my life."

Early felt prickles going up her spine. "Mother, are there things I should know?"

Francie hesitated, her faded blue eyes somewhere far away. "I don't think so. It's just regrets, Earline. I have a passel of them." She looked back, her gaze connecting with Early's. "And I'm afraid, what with this divorce and all, you will, too, and it'll be too late to undo things."

I'm afraid of that, too. And now there was more to fear.

Would she end up as a cranky old person with secrets as her mother had? Should she have fought to sustain her marriage even though Nash so clearly wanted out?

She shook the duster outside, taking a moment to search for another answer. *How can I help my mother, Lord? She hurts in places I don't know about.*

～

"I DON'T UNDERSTAND WHY YOU'RE SO UPSET." SOPHIE FROWNED back at Nash's brooding look. "It's not as if you didn't know you weren't Sarah's father. Why does it matter to you if she finds out who is?"

"Because I *am* her father," he said sharply, "and she's going to get hurt."

Sophie moved toward the stove, brushing lightly against his chest as she passed him. "I'm sorry," she said. "I know you love Sarah just as you do your natural children, but if you ask me, Early's trying to keep you on a husbandly tether, worrying you because Sarah's asking questions."

She put the lid on the stockpot and turned back to face him, her moves studiously lazy, her gaze flirtatious. "Almost ready."

He watched her dispassionately, thinking of Early in her bare feet and cutoff shorts, laughing as she assembled pizzas. And remembering times past when he looked at those shorts and bare feet and wished for languorous movements and sultry looks.

"No," he said quietly, "Early doesn't play games. She's worried about Sarah, just as I am."

"Well." Sophie wasn't so languid now, and her voice was as sharp as his had been. "I think you need to make up your mind. Either you're married or you're not. Your kids are either grown up or they're not. I'm not the wifey kind—you don't have to offer me forever love and loyalty like Early wanted from you—but I don't settle for pieces and parts, either."

He hesitated, feeling tired. Is this what life was all about at this stage? You could either be bored or you could be tired? He'd missed youth's fireworks in his relationship with Early, but he didn't have the patience for the emotional shipwreck of a relationship with Sophie, either.

He liked her, though, liked her deep-throated laugh, her casual approach to life, even her cooking with its unashamed dependence on tomato sauce, olive oil, and lots of cheese. Early'd have a conniption if she knew how much pasta he'd eaten in recent weeks. Or maybe she wouldn't. They'd both been putting effort into becoming people who were not half a couple.

"Okay." He leaned past Sophie to look into the stockpot. "Okay."

He didn't know for sure what he was agreeing to, only that he was too tired to argue. Sarah would be all right. She'd been their little girl all her life; that wasn't about to change. At least, he hoped it wasn't, because he didn't think he could bear that.

CHAPTER 9

IN ALL THE TIME SHE'D BEEN QUILTING, EARLY HAD NEVER BEEN to a quilt show. This year, with her own shop nearly finished, she packed a suitcase with clothes that wouldn't wrinkle, hired a nurse to come in a couple of times a day, and arranged for Mary Brad and numerous family members to see to the feeding of Ben, Francie, and the stray cat Logan and Anna's oldest daughter Abbra had named Clarissa. It was too late for the show in Paducah, Kentucky, but there was one in Vermont that sounded like fun, too.

"Why don't you fly?" Nash demanded, standing in the doorway to her bedroom as she fastened her suitcase. "You can ship anything you buy."

"I'm exhausted, Nash," she said flatly. "I need time alone, time to figure out where life goes from here."

Four weeks in the house with her mother had been difficult. Her last afternoon away had been lunch and grocery-shopping in Pleasant Hill with Mary Brad and that had been two weeks ago. Early had given up manicures and taken to coloring her roots at home after everyone else was in bed.

He nodded. "I can understand that." He stepped into the room to get her luggage. "I'll put this in your car."

The coffee was ready when she went downstairs, as well as a plate with a sandwich and chips on it. She sat at the counter and lifted her cup without meeting Nash's eyes. "Thank you."

He shaped her face with his hand, his expression both somber and smiling as he met her gaze. "Are you sure you won't fly? I promise I won't ask again."

A little while later, fastening her seatbelt, she reflected that no one she knew had ex-husbands who packed their cars for trips, told them numerous times to be careful, and kissed them goodbye. For that matter, they didn't share meals and coffee with the banes of their existence, either.

Of course, that was part of her problem, she thought, turning her car onto the highway and heading north. Nash wasn't the bane of anything. Everything would be much easier if he was.

She drove toward Vermont, realizing with a little thrill that this was the first time she'd taken an overnight trip by herself. It would also be her first time in a hotel without a roommate who squeezed the toothpaste from the middle of the tube and hogged the bed and the remote control.

Divorce wasn't something she'd chosen, and she was still no fan of dating, but Early liked "first times." Life could be much worse.

"WE JUST CAN'T COME DOWN, DAD," SAID LOGAN. "ABBY AND Jacob are broken out with chicken pox now, so you know the other two won't be far behind. And what a way to find out Anna never had them. She feels far worse than the kids do. A multitude of blisters hasn't slowed them down a bit, but she's lying in bed looking like the last rose of summer."

"It's all right. Just take care of your family. We'll be fine here."

By Friday evening, Nash wasn't sure that was true. He had no idea how Early had cared for her mother without going berserk or when his always easy-going father had become so demanding. Mary Brad brought over a pot of vegetable soup Nash personally found delicious, but Francie had complained about the stock being made from Mary Brad's fancy foreign chickens, and Ben said it didn't taste the way Rosie had taught Early to make it.

Because Early always changed all the sheets in the house on Saturday mornings, Nash did, too. What he'd forgotten was that the beds had to be remade, a process that took him a grim half hour. The nurse visited and gave medications while he was making Ben's bed, and she helped him finish. He didn't even mind that she smirked while she did so.

"When I go back to Lexington," he told his father, "remind me to thank all those nursing assistants for working so hard for so little. And for putting up with crusty old geezers at the same time."

"I don't think you should call yourself that, son," said Ben. "From what Evan has said, they call you enough names without you giving them any suggestions."

"I wasn't referring to myself, as you well know. Besides," Nash added, "I don't think you should believe Evan, either. They call him Dr. Darlin'."

Early called on Saturday afternoon while he was pulling burrs from Clarissa's long black fur. "This is fun. I'm getting great ideas," she said. There was so much excitement in her voice he didn't have the heart to tell her he hated the Ridge, hated her mother, and wasn't at all sure how he felt about his father or the cat. "What shall I call my shop?"

"How about A Soft Place to Fall?"

His suggestion fell into silence, and he knew what she was

thinking as well as he knew what train his own mind was jumping onto. That's what their marriage had been until he'd pulled the softness out from under them.

"Maybe." Her voice slipped warm and safe to a place inside him. "Maybe."

"YOU WON'T GET RICH," MARIE COTTON WARNED HER OVER dessert in the hotel restaurant. "You'll be lucky to make a living, and that's if you're so busy you barely take time to eat."

"But you'll always be able to keep your hands in fabric," said Lacey Jackson, her business partner in the Cotton and Lace quilt shop. "And teaching's fun. Sometimes you learn as much as you teach. If you sell sewing or quilting machines, you need to know them inside and out, too. Manufacturing reps are great, but they're not going to be in your store every day."

Early shuddered. "I don't want to sell machines. I can barely keep my own running or operate all their bells and whistles."

"You could rent space in your store to someone who did want to sell them," suggested another woman.

"I'm not ready for that," Early demurred, thinking of the building Noah was constructing on her property. She'd be lucky if she could carve out enough parking for one retail concern, much less two.

"Are any of your children accountants?" Lacey reached for her coffee. "We've found Marie's daughter to be most useful."

Early grinned. "No, but I do have a lawyer in the ranks."

Her mind was going so fast she couldn't sleep when she went to bed. She called Nash. "So? Do you still want to be an investor?"

"Sure." He laughed. "The building's half-done. What are you going to do with it if you don't open a shop?"

She ignored that. "Do you still think it's a good idea?"

"If it's what you want, I think it's a good idea."

"These women know so much and I don't know anything. It's scary."

"But you'll learn it. You learned how to quilt in the first place. Learned about fabric and design and how to operate that long-arm machine that replaced the couch and loveseat in the den." He chuckled. "You never liked Canterbury Crossing, but that room was a good classroom."

"It was," she agreed, thinking of the stacks of books that had graced the den. Nash and Ben had even built a rolling planning wall for her. "I'd like to have a room like that in my shop. For classes and maybe even old-time quilting bees."

He laughed again, and she felt the sound right down to her bare toes. They curled of their own accord against the taut white sheet of the hotel bed. "I can donate medical books, a recliner, and a widescreen TV to the room," he offered, his smile still evident in his voice.

For a moment there was silence as they both remembered the den and the time they'd spent together in it.

How she missed him.

"I was just thinking the other day of how you used to read out loud to me when my eyes got too tired," he said. "That was generous of you when you'd much rather have been reading about quilting or gardening. Sometimes we don't realize our own self-ishness until it's too late to fix it."

"I liked doing it." She closed her eyes and remembered. "It made me feel as though I was an active part of your life. I wasn't educated, couldn't understand the terminology I was reading, couldn't even carry on an intelligent conversation about anything medical other than how to make a bee sting stop throbbing. But I could read to you."

"You were immeasurable help," he said, "and you were always an active part of my life."

Not always, or we wouldn't be where we are now. But she didn't say the words. Their tenuous peace was too precious. "Goodnight, Nash. I'll talk to you later."

Sleepy now, she reflected that they talked more now than they had when they were married.

Life was strange.

"You're worse than the kids when they were little, I swear." Nash glowered at his father and mother-in-law in turn. "Early's been gone five days, and she's had a good time. I can't believe either of you begrudges her that."

"You're a fine one to talk," Ben groused. "You spent thirty years leaving her all the responsibility so you could go off and save the world."

"And she was lucky at that." Francie sniffed. "Not many men made sure their wives had the best appliances and built them houses like that nice one in Lexington. She never was properly grateful. Now she's got this bee in her bonnet about opening a quilt shop." Self-pitying tears fogged her eyes. "Who's going to take care of us?"

Nash opened his mouth to answer, then closed it. Who indeed? He was exhausted after a long weekend. How was Early going to manage a shop *and* their recalcitrant parents? And why was it up to her in the first place?

He was saved from answering his own questions by her arrival.

"It was wonderful." She handed a suitcase to Nash. "I can't wait to stock the shop. I got so many ideas." Her smile moved from Ben to Francie. "You okay? Did Nash keep you fed? Did he take you to rehab?"

"He did," said Francie, "but who's going to take us when you open your store, Earline?"

"You'll be done with rehab by then, Mother, back home and taking care of yourself. You'll be a hundred percent by then, too, Ben, going on Habitat for Humanity builds with your cronies." Early's smile dimmed, but stayed in place. "You'll be okay, won't you?"

"Of course we will, sugar," said Ben. "Now, why don't you leave your luggage for later and sit down and tell us your ideas for a shop?"

Early fixed dinner as she talked, stuffing pita bread with turkey and lettuce and healthy condiments. She made sugar-free pudding from a box, slicing bananas into individual dishes and garnishing them with a stingy sprinkling of graham cracker crumbs and a lone ginger snap.

Nash knew he should pack and prepare to return to Lexington. He needed to stop at the hospital and check on any patients he might have there, and he'd told Sophie he might call her for a late dinner when he got back.

But he didn't. He sat at the table with his ex-wife and their parents and talked and laughed and ate the food that tasted better because Early had prepared it. Afterward, he loaded the dishwasher while his father wiped off the counters and Early displayed samples, fabrics, and ideas on the table.

"It's nonsense, it is, opening a quilt shop way out here in the country." Francie was still complaining, even as she arranged fat eighths with an unerring eye. "You spent all Nash's money making this house just what you wanted, and now you'll never be in it."

"Francie!" Nash spoke sharply. "She worked my way through college and medical school, taking care of the kids the whole time. I'd say she earned any financial settlement she got out of our marriage."

Early smiled faintly at him. They both knew numerous doctors' ex-wives who hadn't fared as well as she had financially, or who had spent copious time in attorneys' offices and court-rooms protecting their investments. It was one of the pitfalls of divorce they'd avoided.

She poured coffee and handed him a cup. "You're a very good ex-husband."

Too little, too late. He shook his head. "Show me your quilt stuff. I may want to invest more."

CHAPTER 10

THE SHOP WAS COZY. SCHOOLHOUSE PLANKED FLOORS WERE
scattered with warm, thick rugs. One could hardly see the cream-
colored walls because it seemed as though every quilter on the
Ridge wanted to hang their work in A Soft Place to Fall. Two cash
registers, big old ones that rang loud with every purchase, perched
at opposite ends of the counter. Early bought them at an auction
and had them cleaned and refurbished.

A coffeepot and an electric teakettle stayed hot all day in
Rosie's Corner, where the window overlooked the creek. There
were sweet things to eat because even before the store was offi-
cially open, the quilters had taken to making extra when they
baked. Ben built a shelf full of pigeonholes just big enough to
hold mugs, so everybody had their own cups. On the wide
windowsill, some of Rosie's salt and pepper shakers provided
color and kindling for conversation.

Fabric was everywhere. Bolts and fat quarters and stacks and
stacks of special cuts. Rolls and packages of batting filled shelves
behind a mobile planning wall. It had taken Early, Mary Brad, and
the girls what seemed like forever to get the colors arranged so
that people looked at the shelves and said, "Ahhh..." when they

entered the store. Only when they asked Francie to supervise the placement did they get it right.

A section of brightly colored batik fabric was called Reginald's, a row of softly flowered calico had been labeled Susan's Garden, and the ceiling-high bay of books and patterns was called the Den. Solid fabrics, jewel-toned but comparatively solemn, were on Jessica's Shelf, and in the corner opposite the coffeepot, with a colorful rug and a small table and chairs, was Sarah's Stuff: crafts specially designed for children whose mothers took way too long in the quilt shop. Juvenile fabric, bright in color and soft to touch, was Anna's Delight. In the middle of the store, necessary but overwhelming to a beginning quilter, was Francie's Rack of Rulers.

A new sewing machine, serger, embroidery machine, and the long-arm quilting machine had a room to themselves. The cost of the equipment had nearly made Early hyperventilate, and she'd crossed a pool off of her mental maybe-list for next summer.

The first time he walked inside the completed shop, Ben's eyes welled with unexpected tears. He hugged Early close. "Rosie would be so proud of you. This was her favorite spot outside the house, and she'd like it even better now."

The grand opening was in mid-October, when fall colors were at their most abundant and as many tourists as locals filled the nearby highway. Jessica, Anna, and Sarah came down for the weekend and donned aprons embroidered with the store logo. "Yes, we're proud of her, but mostly we work cheap," they told customers. Evan and Logan passed out free pins and rulers and carried purchases to people's cars. Two women who'd written several of the books on the shelf in the Den sat at a table and offered autographs and advice.

In Rosie's Corner, customers poured coffee or tea and stayed to add stitches to the Log Cabin quilt on the frame that was set up there. "Come to the soup supper at the little church at the Corners on Saturday after Thanksgiving," Mary Brad advertised. "We're going to auction the quilt there."

Emily Grosvenor, a diplomat who lived in Germany, sent a huge box of fat quarters. "In lieu of wine or flowers," read the card. "Go get 'em, girlfriend."

Nash sent flowers, but didn't attend. Between customers, Early composed a polite thank-you handwritten on store letterhead and tried not to mind that he hadn't come. She tucked a ticket to the soup supper into the envelope with the note.

Josh Walden came with a white basket of roses. He wandered the shop, talking to Early and Noah and Mary Brad, but when Noah introduced him to Sarah as she cut a length of paisley flannel for a customer, all the color drained from Josh's face and he left the store with scarcely a farewell.

"RUNNING THE STORE GIVES ME A NEW APPRECIATION FOR working mothers, that's for sure." Early locked the front door of the shop and turned the closed sign so that it faced the window. "I did it when I was young, but I don't think I could now."

It was the Friday before Thanksgiving and A Soft Place to Fall had been busy ever since the first day it opened. Who knew so many people made quilts for Christmas gifts? Mary Brad, who didn't work Fridays in the law office where she was a paralegal, had taken to spending her days off measuring and cutting fabric.

"Usually there isn't a choice. It's too hard to live on one income. And so many working moms are single. Remember how hard it was for Lou Ann? And she had benefits after John's death." Mary Brad spoke from the restroom beside the machine room, where she was refreshing her makeup.

"I know." Early counted cash and checks into a bank bag. "What are you doing tonight?"

"Riding the Ferris wheel."

They grinned at each other and Early handed Mary Brad the bag for a second count before turning off the lights in the machine room and checking the coffee and tea pots. "Who with?"

Mary Brad finished counting twenties and checked her total with Early's before saying, "Your brother-in-law."

Early felt her eyes widen. "How did Joe accomplish that?"

"He bought tickets to the soup supper for everyone in his office. I was charmed." Mary Brad put the money back into the bag. "How about you, boss lady? What are you doing tonight?"

"Going to dinner and a movie with Josh." Early frowned at her reflection. "I've hardly seen him since we opened." She shrugged. "Of course, I've hardly seen anyone. Even the kids are starting to make cracks about getting appointments and having Thanksgiving dinner catered. Which I don't consider a bad idea, by the way. Oh, and you're invited. Just don't bring anything made with chicken—the grandkids will think it's Reginald."

They left the shop, walking together as far as Mary Brad's car and separating with a brief hug.

Ben had already left to go to supper and a high school basketball scrimmage game with his friends. Francie, looking sorry for herself, sat in front of the living room TV with the remote control in her lap.

Unwilling pity rose under Early's breastbone. "Mother, wouldn't you like to go somewhere?"

"Where?" Both Francie's voice and her expression were sour. "A basketball game at my age? Or out to dinner with you and your fella?"

"He's not my 'fella,' Mother. He's a friend. You have lots of friends, too. Why don't you call and invite them over? Or drive to the Ponderosa and meet them the way you used to? You did just fine driving yourself to the doctor's office the other day, and you hardly even need a cane walking now."

You could go home.

The words lay unspoken between them.

"I'll be all right." Francie gave her a dismissive wave. "You go on."

It reminded Early of her adolescence, when her mother donned a put-upon expression every time Early prepared to leave the house with Nash. Rather than feel guilty, she'd always said, "Come on, Susie. You can go with us."

Years later, when she'd caught herself sighing pathetically as her children prepared to go out, leaving her alone while Nash worked, Early had been drawn up short. She'd started waving them off cheerfully and learned that sometimes her own company wasn't half bad.

But she sighed now, transferring her wallet to a small purse. "I won't be late." The doorbell played the opening bars of "We Gather Together" and she put on a jacket and brushed a kiss over Francie's cheek. "Work on the menu for Thanksgiving, will you?"

She left before her mother could tell her the Thanksgiving menu never varied, and smiled brightly at Josh as they stepped off the porch. "I'm glad to see you. How's school?"

"All right." He opened the car door for her, then went to the other side and got in. "When I was young, I was never ready for the school year to end until April or so, when the kids got antsy and behavior got out of hand. Now I'm ready by the middle of October. I think maybe it's time to retire and sell life insurance."

"I could find a place for you in the shop. Would Noah give you a reference?"

"Probably not. You know how kids are." He reached across the console to squeeze her hand. "I've missed you."

Early realized with a twinge of regret that she hadn't really missed him; she'd been too busy. "Anything new?"

"My daughter's pregnant. Their second one. My son-in-law says it's a boy and that he already likes football and Chevrolets."

"It's amazing what those prenatal tests show, isn't it?" Early laughed. "I wouldn't mind more grandkids, but Logan and Anna have done more than their share and the other three don't seem all that interested in procreating."

"Are they all coming for Thanksgiving?" asked Josh.

"Yes. Normally, this wouldn't be Logan and Anna's year with us, but her parents went to Arizona for the winter and won't be back until March." Early tried not to look gleeful. "If I have to share grandbabies, they're great people to share them with, but I'm greedy about taking all the holidays I can get."

Nash wouldn't be there this year, however, to carve the turkey and help her bake night-before-Thanksgiving pizzas. She wondered if he was spending the day with Sophie, who'd left the practice when Jason returned, but had only gone as far as Frankfort. Far closer than the fifty-seven miles between Lexington and the Ridge.

With an effort she hoped wasn't visible, she brought her attention back to the man at her side. "What are you doing Thanksgiving?"

"Going to my daughter's in Louisville. Rebecca takes the holiday entertainment of her widowed father very seriously."

Their conversation was friendly, but not particularly comfortable. Early wanted to ask him why he'd left the shop so abruptly the weekend of its grand opening, but their unease with each other held her back. She thought of Sarah and Nash's relationship and wondered if she was simply afraid to hear Josh's answers.

But after they'd eaten dinner at the new restaurant that had opened in Stringtown Proper and were lingering over pie and coffee, Early swallowed trepidation. "Josh, did you know my sister?"

He hesitated, stirring half and half into his coffee and giving it an inordinate amount of attention. "Yes." He laid the spoon beside his plate. "I didn't remember she was your sister until I saw your younger daughter at the store, but then I knew it had to be." He cleared his throat. "She looks just like her, doesn't she?"

"Yes, she does, only Sarah's hair is red and Susie's was blonde." Early waited. Surely he would tell her how he'd known Susan. Wouldn't he? Well, unless he'd known her better than he wanted to admit.

The restaurant wasn't at all quiet, but she felt as though she were speaking into dead silence. "Were you with her?"

He sighed, looking away. "No, though not because of any nobility on my part, I have to admit. Three of us were down at Little Cat, fishing, when she came down. She was...you know how she was."

Early closed her eyes, remembering Susie's innocence. "Yes."

"Do you remember who else was there? What stopped you from taking advantage of the situation?" She knew the words sounded harsh, but someone had hurt Susie.

"Joe McGrath."

"Nash's brother?" Like there'd been another Joe McGrath on the Ridge. Or anywhere. McGrath men tended to be one of a kind. But Joe wouldn't have hurt Susie.

"It was Frank and Kyle Lambert and I who were there." Josh stirred his coffee again, his handsome face reddening. "Joe got between her and us. The Lamberts were ready to fight him to get to her, but I didn't have the stomach for three-to-one odds. Besides, I knew anything I did to Joe, Nash would do to me later twice over."

Early nodded agreement, smiling. "He would have, too."

"I was at the University of Louisville by then," Josh continued. "I used to see Susie down at the creek when I was home. I always had studying to do and I'd do it aloud. It helped me to remember what I read and she was a rapt audience. She was so sweet, and I think she liked the attention from someone who didn't want anything from her." He shook his head. "I just feel so guilty, and have for years, because I knew things that happened to her and I didn't do anything about it. Not the first thing."

Early shook her head. "You couldn't have watched her all the time. We tried. It didn't work."

"When I got married, I left the Ridge and never looked back other than to visit every couple of years. When Jackie first got sick, though, we wanted to be closer to family. There was no one left in Michigan, so we came here."

He sipped his coffee. "Life was hard there for a while. I still miss Jackie every day, though I've stopped looking for her every time I open my eyes. And it's nice, you know, seeing people that I knew back then. But I hadn't thought of Susie in years. When I saw Sarah, it was a shock, and I felt guilty all over again."

"I don't remember the Lamberts," Early commented, trying to place the name.

"They moved back to Over Yonder while we were in high school. Their folks were from there, I think. Anyway, the boys got drunk one night when I was in college and drove their car off the bridge over Big Cat after they robbed Davis's gas station. Kyle went to jail for a while and Frank was badly injured. A few years later, Kyle was killed in the coal mine accident."

Early remembered standing in the rain with Mary Brad and Lou Ann on the day their husbands' bodies were brought out of the mine, having no words of comfort to offer, only her presence. Among those waiting had been a man in a wheelchair, a man with red hair and angry eyes.

She hadn't thought anything about it then—there'd been a lot of anger in the crowd that day—but now she wondered. Who was the man with red hair and how well had he known Susan?

"Do you know," she asked, "if they went back to...visit Susie?"

He shook his head. "Not that I know of, but I never saw them after high school. I went to the funeral home when Kyle died, but I went to John Hendry's and Paul Hardesty's viewings, too, and I don't remember much about any of them."

Early remembered them far too well. She and the kids had driven from Lexington to the Ridge every day for two weeks after the men's deaths. They'd stayed with Lou Ann's children during the day while their mother did the things she had to do and spent evenings with Mary Brad.

Nash had waited up for her each night, coming outside to help carry the sleeping children into the house and put them in their beds. He had the coffee ready and sat and held her close while the pain of the day settled down to a point where she could bear it.

He'd been a soft place to fall long before it had become either a popular phrase or the name of a quilt shop.

"I wish I had some information that might help." Regret lay hard across Josh's features. "Sarah's as lovely as her mother was."

"She is."

As a date, the evening didn't even come close to being a success. "I'm sorry to be such terrible company," Early said when he pulled into her driveway. She met his eyes across the width of the front seat. "My mind's going in too many directions right now."

"It's all right. Mine is, too." He stroked a finger down the side of her face. "You thought I might be Sarah's father."

"I did." She sighed. "I'm glad you're not, because that would have complicated things for everyone. I can't imagine how your children would feel. But I still wonder who is, for Sarah's sake."

"Well, not to muddy the waters," he said, "but why don't you talk to Joe? Not that he's her father, but he might know something that would help. For that matter, I'd be willing to do DNA testing."

Early must have looked as horrified as that statement made her feel.

"Not that there's a reason. Just so it doesn't look like you're singling out Lambert. He's not the nicest person to deal with."

She took a deep breath. "You want to come in? I've got some cider Mother mulled today."

"Not tonight. I'm spending the weekend with Noah because he won't be with us for Thanksgiving, and we're going to drive south until it's warm enough to play golf."

There was a strange sort of finality to their goodnights, and mixed with the regret, Early felt a little relief she didn't fully understand.

Inside, she got ready for bed, deciding it wouldn't hurt her to sleep in makeup just this once, and wandered into the kitchen. She poured a glass of milk, then went to lie in bed and stare blindly at the television.

Her life as a single woman was taking shape. Good shape. Although caring for aging parents wasn't something she would have chosen, it had become manageable. The shop, while it required hard work and long hours, was a joy and a satisfaction. Loneliness was...well, what it was. Most everyone was lonesome at one time or another. She even had a few clues as to who Sarah's birth father may have been. So why did Early feel so unsettled?

"Thank You for Your blessings, for Your constancy and Your love…"

Her faith was simple: with prayer came peace. However, tonight there was an unfinished feeling. "What do You want me to do, Lord? What am I missing?"

Finally, she picked up the phone and hit the speed dial button for the familiar number. "I'm sorry I didn't ask earlier," she told Nash's answering machine, "but if you haven't planned anything for Thanksgiving, we'd be glad to have you. I could use help with pizza on Wednesday night." She hesitated. "I need to talk to you about something, and then I'd like for us to talk to Joe."

CHAPTER 11

"IF NO ONE LIKES IT, I DON'T SEE WHY WE HAVE IT." SARAH PUT the can of jellied cranberry sauce back on the pantry shelf, placing it behind the oatmeal box in a gesture everyone knew was doomed to fail.

"Because it's tradition, and it looks pretty on the glass dish Grandpa won for Grandma Rosie at the fair." Jessie answered her sister's complaint without even looking up from the pizza dough she was kneading.

"I could swear I've heard this same conversation ever since you could talk, Sarah," said Evan, reaching around her for a bag of potato chips. He tossed the chips onto the counter and leaned over to pluck Logan and Anna's youngest from where she was intent on clearing the bottom pantry shelf. "I thought you were throwing this one back because she was puny," he told his brother. He lifted little Fiona and blew on her belly like the expert uncle he was. She shrieked and giggled and kicked him with tiny baby feet.

"Nah. Mom and Dad kept you. Lowered the bar for the whole family." Logan exchanged grins with his daughter. "And Anna likes her."

"Anna likes everyone, even you two." Sarah walked between her brothers, taking Fiona with her. "Come on, baby Fee, let's go polish your toenails. If Grandpa Nash is asleep on the couch, we'll do his, too."

"Do Dad's in blue," Jessie suggested. "He needs some color in his life."

Early shook her head. "Finish the crusts, Jessica Darcy." She bent to get the pizza pans out of the cupboard in the island, leaving the door open for Fiona's eleven-months-older brother to climb inside. "Nash," she called over the noise of her delightfully full house, "are you going to help with these pizzas or are you going to leave our digestive tracts to the tender mercies of the kids?"

"Be right there."

He followed his voice into the kitchen. His hair was rumpled, his glasses askew on his face, and he wore lipstick and bilious blue eye shadow. He slowed when everyone stopped what they were doing to look at him. "What?"

"You should have worn the green, Dad. It looks better with your eyes," said Logan. "And you should never fall asleep with your oldest granddaughter in the house. Abby likes to play with makeup."

"Not the first time that's happened." Nash gave Jessie's hair a tug. "Francie's asleep in the chair in there. What do you suppose she'll look like?"

"Herself." Logan got a board game from the cabinet above the refrigerator. "The kids are afraid of her, so they won't bother her." He looked hard at his father's face. "They must think you're an absolute pussycat, Dad. No fear at all."

"I'll be back after I wash my face." Nash smiled at Early.

She smiled back before he walked away, thinking that the exchange of an expression could replace an entire conversation between people who'd known each other for a long time.

After dinner, which was loud, hilarious, and messy, everyone went in different directions. Evan and Logan played dominoes with Ben. Jessie went home with Noah. Sarah and Anna put the children to bed and went down to the shop with Francie. Joe walked Mary Brad home, then came into the kitchen where Nash was loading the dishwasher while Early baked cookies.

"So," said Joe, going to the coffeepot, "what did you want to talk to me about, Early? I've already palmed my father and my brother off on you. There's nothing more I can do to you."

They sat at the table, a plate of warm cookies on its center lazy Susan, and Early gave them the *Reader's Digest* version of her conversation with Josh, leaving out Joe's involvement. When she was finished, she looked over at her brother-in-law, trying to tune out the anger she felt emanating from Nash. "Do you know the Lamberts?" she asked.

Joe, who'd been reaching for a cookie, drew his hand back. "I do," he said. "Or I did. Kyle's dead, and I haven't seen Frank in years. I'm not sure he's still alive."

"He is." She'd made sure of that.

Nash frowned. "How do you know them?"

"Frank was a client. When his brother was killed in the mine explosion, he was part of the class action suit. Kyle was his only source of support."

That wasn't the answer Early had expected. "You knew them before, too, didn't you?"

"Early, where are you going with this?" he asked. "It can't do anyone any good."

"Come on, Joe, answer the question," Nash said impatiently. "Did you know them before?"

"I met them once." Joe sighed. "Twice. I met them twice."

"The first time when you stopped them from hurting Susie," Early said.

He looked surprised, but only slightly. "Yes."

"And after that?" Nash prodded.

Joe hesitated, and his eyes got that haunted look Nash's had after he lost a patient. "After that," he said finally, "when I got there too late to stop them."

"Why didn't you ever tell us?" Early cried, anger rising up like a storm inside her. "You knew Sarah would eventually want to know her biological history."

"Tell you what, Early?" Joe's voice was quiet, but there was torment in his dark eyes. "You know how Susie was. Would it have made you feel better to know the name of everyone who took advantage of her? She wasn't raped, not in the physical sense. In the emotional and mental sense, of course she was. But what good would it have done to tell you?"

"Is one of the Lamberts Sarah's father?" asked Nash.

Joe hesitated. "I don't know. Frank's hair was red like Sarah's is, but that's not enough to base a paternity suit on. She's the spit and image of Susan, with a little bit of Early thrown in for strength." He leaned forward, meeting Early's gaze. "Sarah is Nash's daughter as much as Jessie is, as much a McGrath as any of us. Why can't you leave it at that?"

"I can," she said, "and I think Nash can, too"—his nod affirmed her statement—"but I'm not so sure Sarah can."

"I'm afraid she'll get hurt."

Nash's smile was slight and lopsided, but still there. "So are we. We'll take care of our own, Joe, but we need to find this out for Sarah's sake. Early says Josh Walden has offered to be part of the testing, just so it won't appear as though we're pointing fingers only at the Lamberts."

"That would be a smoke screen," argued his brother. "Pointless. And just say Frank *is* her father. There's no possible way that could be a good thing. He's the personification of every hill-country stereotype we've ever heard of. He's mean and he's a drunk. He could work, but as far as I know never has.

You may have a slew of shortcomings, but you're a good father."

"Look at who's mentioning shortcomings," Nash said scornfully. "Shall we talk to any of your ex-wives about them? We all know DNA doesn't promise you stellar siblings, but it is a resource for health information in case of an emergency."

"Stellar siblings," said Joe. "Whoa, big brother, getting downright pompous, aren't we?"

"Stop it, both of you," scolded Early. "This isn't about you. It's about Sarah. She doesn't have to have a relationship with her biological father. I'm pretty sure she's not looking for any more male relatives. She does need to know if she enters into a relationship with someone, he's not going to end up being her halfbrother."

"I don't think John David Hendry poses a problem," said Joe.

His brother gave him a hard glance. "We don't know she's going to spend the rest of her life with John David. You're living testimony to the permanency of relationships."

Joe scowled back at him. "You're not doing so well in that area yourself, now, are you?"

Early sighed. "All right, we may as well give this up as a lost cause. The McGrath boys would rather argue between themselves than be helpful. Goodnight."

Silence fell between her ex-husband and his brother. She got up and went to bed, not particularly caring what they did and glad she didn't have to worry about it. Nash's relationship with his brother wasn't even remotely her responsibility.

Freedom.

The word struck her as she slipped into flannel pajama pants and a matching tee shirt worn faded and soft from washing. She went to the French doors and stepped out onto the porch, staring into the woods.

She was no longer married to Nash McGrath, but she had

the best parts of him anyway: his children, his family, and his friendship. She was finished rearing her children; was not a counted-on-to-babysit Nana to Logan and Anna's little ones, but she still had all of them to love and enjoy. She had her own home, which with all of its jutting-out additions and odd room arrangements was probably an architectural nightmare but suited her right down to the ground. She owned her business and was not limited by the nuances of city zoning and ordinance.

Even though her house was full to its rafters, with someone sleeping in nearly every room, when all was said and done, she was alone. Ben and Francie lived in the house with her and the three of them were related but not a family unit. No, the family unit, whether she had chosen it or not, was Early. Alone and free.

She wasn't sure yet, but she thought she liked it.

NASH AND JOE CAME OUT OF THE WOODS TOGETHER THE NEXT morning while Early stood at the sink washing the interior of the turkey. The men carried coffee cups and wore hooded sweatshirts against the November chill.

As they approached the back porch, Joe said something and Nash threw back his head and laughed aloud. Early stood frozen in place, the bag of turkey giblets forgotten in her hand. After a moment, she forced herself to breathe.

It would always be this way, she supposed, tossing them a brief smile when they came into the house. Even as she began to feel at home in her new life, the sight, touch, and scent of Nash would always throw her into an emotional tailspin of one sort of another.

"I'll talk to Frank," said Joe without preamble as he approached the table, "if that's what you want me to do, Early.

But it won't be necessary for Josh to do the test. I don't particularly care if Frank Lambert feels picked on."

"I appreciate it, and Josh probably will, too." She smiled at
Joe again. "You know, there for a while I hoped it was you.
Somehow that would have been all right, because Susie loved you
and Sarah loves you, too. But it wouldn't have been all right for
you, would it?"

"No. I loved Susie, but I couldn't have touched her, even
without knowing Nash would kill me. She was just too much like
a sister for me to think that way about. Plus, even though she was
handicapped, she was almost four years older than I was. At that
age, four years seemed like a lifetime of difference." A flash of
sadness crossed his face. "Doesn't mean I wouldn't welcome the
idea of Sarah being mine, though. I do love that child."

"So where were you when she became our fourth kid in
college at one time?" asked Nash, snagging the coffee carafe and
refilling all their cups. "Remember, Early? All we did was write
checks to educational institutions."

"That's all *you* did," she corrected, thumping the turkey onto
the island and reaching for the bowl of stuffing. "I did laundry. I
don't think any of them washed their own clothes until they'd
gotten their master's degrees."

"Logan did. He got married," said Joe.

Nash nodded, taking pans of raised cinnamon rolls from the
top of the refrigerator. "And a good job he did of it, too. These
ready to bake, Early?"

"Set the timer for twenty minutes, please, or the boys will be
playing Frisbee with them. Anna did Logan's laundry when they
got married, though. I don't think he opened the washer lid until
she was knee-deep in nursing school and toddlers. You want to
make more coffee, Joe? I hear stirrings from all parts of the
house."

It was the best kind of family day. John David brought extra tables and chairs from the church basement so everyone was able to sit and eat at one time, albeit there was no room left for unnecessary movement. Mid-afternoon, the children took naps, the men settled in front of the TV for football, and the women went down to the quilt shop, gathering around the large frame to stitch and talk.

"This is a nice thing you've done here, Early," said Francie.

Early was rolling the auction quilt onto a long cardboard cylinder for its trip to the church. "What's that, Mother?" she asked absently.

"The shop. What it's done for the women on the Ridge. Rena Calloway sold her double wedding ring quilt for enough to pretty near pay a semester's tuition for her boy and you wouldn't take a dime even though you hung it here in the store. It was generous of you and a good thing. And that little Angie Fairchild comes in here every day after her little girls get on the bus. She walks nigh onto two miles to get here, but she knows her man won't find her and beat on her. She sits and stitches and doesn't talk to anyone, but she knows she's safe." Francie pushed her needle in and out in perfectly uniform stitches. "I'm right proud of you."

"We are, too, Mama." Jessie sewed as perfectly as her grandmother, but about a third as fast.

"All of us," Sarah agreed, frowning down at the quilt top. "Why is it that Anna and I are the girliest ones here and we have the worst looking stitches?"

"Not the worst," Mary Brad said. "Those would be mine."

"Doesn't matter." Early wrapped the rolled quilt loosely in muslin. "It's a work of love. If art is sacrificed, it's okay with me."

She came over and looked down at the five pairs of hands stitching the quilt top. She could see their ages, their histories. Francie's were spotted and gnarled with the effects of age and arthritis, and fifteen years after she'd stopped wearing her wedding ring, its shape was still obvious on her left hand. Mary Brad's were thin but strong with her right little finger gone from the second knuckle, the result of a long-ago accident. Jessie's hands were short and sturdy like Early's own, Sarah's as long and slim as Susan's had been. Anna's fell somewhere between the girls' in shape and size, just as she herself did in the family: a good fit.

Logan called the shop an hour or so later to tell Anna the children were awake but they were fine, so Mary Brad made fresh coffee and they continued to sew as the shadows lengthened outside. Eventually noise made them go to the front windows. The men were in the yard between the shop and the house, playing football. The children ran among them, even little Fiona, whose feet were often outrun by the rest of her.

The other women went back to the quilt—they were almost done—but Early stayed where she was, not wanting anyone to see the tears that slipped silent and warm down her cheeks. The moment was like the quilt and the hands that stitched it. The men differed as much as the women did, yet they came together to play a game and dote on the little ones, picking up Lucas and Fiona as they ran and tossing Abby and Jacob into the piles of leaves. Like the quilt and the hands, with all their flaws, the tableau in the yard was perfect.

Is this Your answer, Lord?

"I'm going to go set stuff out," she said, and stepped outside.

Fiona toddled over, and she swung her to her hip, nuzzling her neck and smelling the sweet scent of baby. "Food in ten minutes," she called.

Nash, with Lucas on his back, joined her for the walk to the house. "I'll help," he offered. "There is pie left, right? The pumpkin one that Evan and Logan split wasn't the last one?"

"No, but the one you and Joe and Ben chowed down at halftime might have been."

"How'd you know about that?" he asked, holding the door open for her to enter the kitchen.

She grinned up at him. "We may not be married anymore, but things haven't changed that much."

"Put me down, Grandpa," ordered Lucas suddenly. "I gots to *go.*"

"Go for it, youngun." Nash let the boy slide to the floor, his gaze never leaving Early's face. "Why were you crying?"

Her first thought was to deny it, but he knew her too well for that, so she just smiled at him again. "For the first time in longer than I care to think about, I was crying happy." She took a deep breath. "It grieves me to admit it, but our separation was probably a good thing. I guess I had to lose you to find myself."

THE AUCTION QUILT WAS PURCHASED BY A YOUNG WOMAN WHO'D come from Lexington to visit A Soft Place to Fall and bought soup supper tickets on her way out the door. Maggie Bentley had been so pleased with the store that she'd come back and brought her friends, and so hopeful of getting the quilt that she'd brought even more friends to the soup supper.

"If I bring five of my friends down one day a week, will you do a class?" she asked Early.

"Of course, but after Christmas. We can do it in two sessions, morning and afternoon. I'll provide lunch if you like, but the fee will be higher."

"Wonderful!" Maggie gave a gleeful little squeal. "Oh, excuse me. I have to find my kids before they create a new baptistery in the men's restroom."

Early laughed. "It wouldn't be the first time, believe me."

By the time she got home from her two-hour stint at the church, Ben had gone to the basketball game with his friends and

Francie was playing cards with hers. The house was silent when Early entered it. She checked her messages, made a cup of hot chocolate and a bowl of popcorn, and curled up on the couch with a new book. Clarissa sat at her feet, applying an industrious tongue to Early's fuzzy socks.

The phone rang, and she gave serious thought to letting the machine answer, but curiosity won out and she picked it up on the third ring.

"I'm sorry I couldn't come. Who got the quilt?" asked Nash.

"Oh." Early chuckled. "Maggie Bentley. She lives in Canterbury Crossing, and she and Anna are friends. The world certainly has shrunk."

"Sure has. She's a patient of Evan's. Or was. I think she switched over to Jason after the first time she and Evan ran into each other outside the office."

"Ran into each other?"

"Uh-huh. It was amazing. Then Evan suddenly started visiting Logan and Anna a couple of times a week instead of just a catch-up lunch with Logan once in a while. Anna and I have been taking bets. I think it's the real thing but Anna says not."

A little billow—less than a full wave—of resentment washed over Early. *She* was the mom, wasn't she? *She* was the one who always knew more about the kids' lives than Nash did, who talked to them late at night over hot chocolate and cookies straight from the oven. Their father had always been too busy to keep up, so she'd had to update him during their time alone.

"Do you ever think about just us?" he'd asked once, interrupting her narrative on the girls' prom dresses.

She didn't answer right away, and he said, "Never mind. Forget it."

And so she had. Until now.

"I'm sorry," she said suddenly, interrupting whatever he was saying. "Nash, I'm sorry."

"Well, I'm certain I'm going to forgive you," he said, "as soon as you tell me what it is you're sorry about."

"I never..." She stopped, uncertain how to go on. "I felt so righteous," she said, "because it was always family first for me. Nothing ever got in the way of that. Including marriage. You and the kids are...you were a package deal. I didn't...I think I didn't always make the marriage as important as I should have."

"Oh." He was silent for a moment. "I can compartmentalize. It's something you learn in medical school when you're too tired to absorb everything you need to. So it's easy for me to think of one child at a time, to think of you and me separately from them. You thrive on the full, loud house and grieve when they all go home. I like having everyone together, too, but after a day of it, I'm on sensory overload because I can't divide myself neatly between everyone when there are that many. You have a generous soul that doesn't require division. Don't ever apologize for that."

"But I should have—"

"No more 'should haves.' We're too old for that."

"Good night, Nash."

"Sleep warm, Early."

CHAPTER 12

NASH AND HIS BROTHER RODE DOWN TOGETHER IN JOE'S CAR, something they never did. They both left work early, something they seldom did. They rode the entire fifty-seven miles without arguing over anything, something they hadn't done nearly often enough. They talked about weather, about football, about how great their father looked. In tacit agreement, they *didn't* talk about why they were going to Early's on the second Friday in December. That would wait until they arrived. As he walked with his younger brother into Early's house, Nash felt a stab of regret that they weren't closer. *Was it me all the time, Lord, when I blamed him and his lifestyle because we couldn't connect?*

Joe hung his coat over the back of a chair and spoke without preamble, laying a brown interoffice message envelope on the kitchen table. "It was Frank."

For a long and silent shriek in time, they all stared at the envelope. Nash cleared his throat. "Well."

Early sat down so suddenly, he and Joe both made a move to catch her. Her face was ghostly white, the freckles across her nose seeming to stand out in bas relief. She set the coffee carafe on the table and stared down at it. "What now?"

"I don't know," said Joe. "I haven't talked to Lambert about it, nor do I particularly want to. The very idea of Sarah even having to meet him makes me want to puke."

Still holding the handle of the pot, Early looked up at them. "I thought finding out was the right thing, but now that we have, I'm afraid it was a mistake."

Joe got cups and brought them to the table. Early filled them automatically. She even smiled at Joe and gestured for him to take a seat at the table, but Nash was pretty sure she wasn't really seeing his brother. She was seeing a red-haired man in a wheelchair who had changed Susan's life and might be able to change Sarah's, too.

Nash took the carafe back to the coffeemaker's keep-warm plate. "I don't know." He shared a humorless look with her. "I'm all for burning the envelope and forgetting the whole thing."

They were interrupted by the doorbell playing "Deck the Halls," followed by a call from the living room. "Mama? Daddy? Are you both here?"

Nash sighed silently. As much as he loved his children, he didn't feel up to spending the evening with any of them. Even when an emotional upheaval was positive—and he was pretty sure this one wasn't—it was also wearing, and he was exhausted.

"In here, Sarah." Early relegated the brown envelope to a drawer in the island.

Sarah and Jessica came into the kitchen, followed by John David and Noah. "Hi, Uncle Joe." The girls kissed them all. "What're y'all doing?" asked Sarah.

There was an air of suppressed excitement about her that had her parents exchanging looks. They stepped closer together, their shoulders touching. "Not a lot," Nash said. "What about you? Did you play hooky today, Sarah?"

"No, Daddy, but I did take the afternoon off. John David and I had plans."

"We just came along for the ride, and maybe for Friday-night pizza." Jessie grinned, her McGrath dimples flashing.

Nash and Early exchanged another look. Plans? Sarah never "took the afternoon off." Her students, emotionally handicapped kindergarten through third-graders, were always upset by her absence.

"Since you're both here." John David's easygoing eloquence seemed to have left him. There was a tremor in his voice and—in mid-December, fresh from the outdoors—he appeared to be perspiring.

"You want some coffee, son?" asked Joe. "And would you like me to leave the room?"

"No, sir. I'd like to say this quick, if it's all right, and I don't really mind who's here as long as Nash and Miss Early are."

Nash nodded at him. "By all means." He reached for Early's hand, and she laced her fingers through his.

How right that still felt. They'd never been overtly affectionate; they'd gone days without exchanging more than the most perfunctory of kisses. But they'd always felt good to each other, had always been able to count on the love they shared. Oddly enough, he still counted on that.

"We understand that we haven't been seeing each other very long," said the young minister earnestly, drawing Sarah close to his side, "but losing my parents made me understand the importance of living every day like it was the only day. So, whether we have just the one or, God willing, sixty years of days, we'd like to spend them together. We want to be married, and we'd like to do it with your blessing."

"You have it." Nash's and Early's voices came out as one, and Nash thought maybe his fingers cracked when she squeezed them.

A great deal of hugging and back-thumping followed. Francie came in from the quilt shop and Ben came home from a Habitat for Humanity meeting and even Francie melted enough to hug her least-favored grandchild in congratulations.

"We'll wait till the end of the school year," said Sarah, "and get married here in John David's church in June." Her eyes, the same washed blue her mother's had been, were star-bright when she looked up at Nash. "Will you give me away, Daddy?"

Nash felt his throat close up. He reached for Sarah, folding her close. "I'll loan you out," he managed to say, "but I'm not giving you away to anybody." He met John David's eyes over her bright hair. "That work for you?"

"Yes, sir." The younger man extended his hand. "I'll share her and I'll care for her," he said with old-fashioned formality.

Nash shook his hand and responded in kind. "That's all her mother and I ask." He reached for Early's hand again, wanting her at his side.

"Well, actually," Early said, "I ask more than that. Grandchildren would be excellent. Just one of each for me and then you can have more for yourselves if you like."

"We'll do our best," Sarah promised.

The girls went to A Soft Place to Fall with their mother to work the last hour before closing, giving Francie a chance to put her feet up in the living room before dinner.

Even with only part of the family there, it was noisy. The kitchen congested as they prepared pizzas and talked about wedding plans. Nash was tempted to go back to Lexington with the kids, but he wanted to talk to Early alone and the truth was that he didn't feel all that well. Jason had held him still for a blood pressure check that morning, then commandeered a technician from the lab to draw blood.

"You're not looking great." His partner spoke with the bluntness of long friendship. "Let's talk to Sophie about coming up here for a couple of months. She did fine with my patients and she's about done in Frankfort. You need the time off."

The younger generation headed to Lexington after dinner. Joe walked through the woods to Mary Brad's. Ben and Francie went to their rooms.

Nash felt Early's gaze on him as they loaded the dishwasher. "I don't like it when the kids are on the road," she said. "It's too much like when they were in high school."

"It's when we have to remind ourselves that they're grownups."

"I don't know about that. They still got out of doing the dishes." She laughed, but she was still watching him. "Nash?" Her hand was there again, shaping his face with soft coolness. "Are you all right?"

"Yeah." He forced a smile. "Tired. I still feel about seventeen, but whether I like it or not, the body's pushing fifty."

Her gaze held his, the heat in her eyes blending nicely with the coolness of her touch. "Do you want to spend the weekend?" she asked. "You rest well here, don't you? And the guest room's always ready. The real room, I mean, not the inflatable beds and foldout couches. You probably have a weekend's worth of clothes here."

He thought for a minute, remembering that he and Sophie were supposed to go to dinner and a play tomorrow night. She was driving over to Lexington. It was really too late to cancel.

And he was pretty much too tired to care.

"If you wouldn't mind," he said to Early, "I'd like to stay. I need to make a few calls to clear up the weekend."

"Go ahead. Do you want some hot chocolate? I always make some for Mother and Ben."

"That would be good."

He went outside to make his phone calls. Even though the divorce was a long time final, he couldn't bring himself to call Sophie from Early's house.

Sophie was angry, and he couldn't blame her. "Let's see,

you're breaking a date with me to spend the weekend with your ex-wife. What's wrong with that picture?" Sarcasm dripped from her voice.

"I'm sorry," he said honestly, "but I'm whipped. I need some down time, and the Ridge is the best place to get that."

"The Ridge or with Earline?" Her voice rose on the last syllable of Early's name in a nasal attempt at an Eastern Kentucky accent.

Suddenly, he didn't care if she was angry or not. "Maybe both," he said crisply. "So long, Sophie." He hung up.

And then he called Jason.

EARLY WANDERED THE HOUSE AT NIGHT JUST AS SHE HAD WHEN the kids lived at home. She did it to check their breathing when they were small—one story of sudden infant death syndrome was all she'd needed to hear. Then she progressed to sitting on the beds and listening to the stories kids tell only at night when their fears are at their deepest. Later, she would wake from a sound sleep to see who was late for curfew. Often she had sat at the table with Nash, home late from being on call. There had been times after a patient died that they'd sat there all night, drinking coffee and making desultory conversation until he could bear the loss.

It was prayer time. Francie had always read her Bible and devotions sitting in her chair with her morning coffee. The girls had known not to disturb her until she was finished. But Early had done her private praying sitting on the stairs. She still did.

Now she made her nighttime rounds to make sure Ben and Francie were resting, that they'd taken their before-bed medications. Sometimes Ben wanted to talk about Rosie. A couple of times, early in her stay, Francie cried and Early offered awkward comfort.

Tonight, both of them slept. Early went into the kitchen and made a pot of decaf. She hadn't learned to like it as much as caffeinated coffee, but it fit into the cup just as well.

She retrieved Joe's brown envelope from the drawer and sat at the table to peruse its contents. The reports made no sense to her, but they didn't have to. It was enough to know Frank Lambert had fathered Sarah.

Oh, God, what now? Why did I even start this? She thought of the closeness between Sarah and Nash. Would this undermine it? Would Sarah want to meet the man in the wheelchair? Being compassionate right down to the marrow of her bones, would she name him as her father? If she did, what would that do to Nash, the man who was her father every way but genetically?

Early's head pounded with the questions. The answers. The possibilities.

She got up, putting the envelope back in the drawer and moving restlessly through the downstairs rooms. It always felt better, she admitted reluctantly to herself, when Nash was in the house. She'd lived with him for thirty years; she still felt safer in his presence than at any other time.

But tonight felt strange. Off. The girls had gotten home safely; she'd talked to both Evan and Logan today; Francie and Ben were well. The brown envelope was…well, just an envelope.

She sipped her coffee and went into the sewing room, plugging in the small Christmas tree in the corner and sitting on the love seat to watch the twinkling lights. She missed sitting outside, but it had gotten too cold for that, so the multi-windowed room was a good substitute.

"Early?"

She looked up at the sound of Nash's voice.

"Can't sleep?"

"I did. I just woke up."

He looked better, though, more rested, and she felt relief slip under her skin. Maybe she was imagining things. "There's decaf in the kitchen."

"Good. Need a warmup?"

A minute later, he returned with both cups full, handing her one and sitting on the other half of the love seat, his bare feet joining hers on the ottoman in front of it. "Pretty tree," he said. "How many do you have?"

She grinned. Her love for Christmas trees had been a family joke for years. "Six, not counting the ones in the shop. If I'd known you were coming, I'd have gotten one for the guest room. Ben says the one in his room drives him nuts, but he always turns it on as soon as he goes in there."

"You've made a great home here." He looked around the inviting room. "I know this is the time of glass and metal and sharp corners, but there's always comfort to be found in whatever your style is. Mom would love it."

Early laughed. "She taught me her style of decorating; you know, as in if I like it, I use it."

He put his arm around her, drawing her to him, and she went willingly, cozying her head into his shoulder.

HE LOVED HOW SHE LOOKED.

Nash didn't want to admit even to himself that he hadn't always, that he'd grown so used to the sheer ordinariness of Early's looks that he hadn't really looked at her anymore.

"Mama looks tired," Sarah had said on Thanksgiving. "She does too much."

Nash had looked from his daughter to his ex-wife in surprise and seen that Sarah was right. The lines around Early's eyes had deepened over the eventful autumn and her summer-in-the-flowerbeds tan had faded, leaving her too pale.

But then Evan had muttered something undeniably rude and John David said, "Oh, dear Lord, forgive him, and me, too, for laughing so hard," and Early burst into laughter.

She didn't look all that tired anymore, and certainly not ordinary.

Two weeks later, she still didn't look ordinary to him, but the weariness had dipped all the way to complete exhaustion. Being in the retail business between Thanksgiving and Christmas, she said, was not for the weak.

Neither was hearing the contents of that envelope. He wondered if it bothered her as much as it did him.

She wore plaid pajama pants with a faded tee shirt and fuzzy socks on her feet. Her hair was flat on one side and her face was devoid of makeup. He was reminded, as she gazed at the Christmas tree with sleepy gray eyes, of the nights when she sat up breastfeeding their babies. She'd been this kind of tired then, too, with an alluring softness to her he'd been completely unable to resist even if he'd wanted to.

"Hey," he said now, and then didn't remember what he'd meant to tell her, because he kissed her instead. He sighed. "Oh, Early."

Her lips moved against his. "I know," she said. "I know."

He cleared his throat. "We need to talk about Sarah."

CHAPTER 13

"Would it have been harder for you," Nash asked, "if Josh Walden had been Sarah's father?"

The oven timer dinged behind Early and she rose quickly to pull the pan of cinnamon rolls from the oven. She set them on the counter in front of Nash and snipped a corner from a sandwich bag full of icing. "Here, drizzle this over the rolls."

She took lasagna out of the refrigerator and put it in the still-hot oven, resetting the timer before she sat down again. She'd never asked him any details about Sophie Donato, never commented when he went outside to make phone calls. Just as she would never call Josh from Nash's home, she was sure he wouldn't call Sophie from hers. She'd never particularly liked the other woman, a feeling she was certain was reciprocated, but she hadn't disliked her, either. At least not until Nash had started seeing her and Early had spent a few wakeful nighttime hours worrying that the beautiful doctor would be her children's step-mother. But that hadn't been her primary reason for not asking.

No, the real reason was that she hadn't wanted to know.

"Do you really want to ask me that?" she said now. It wasn't as if she had anything to hide—the relationship with Josh had never progressed beyond what they would have described in their younger days as "first base"—but the truth was that it wasn't any of Nash's business. Just as Sophie Donato wasn't any of hers.

He laughed, though there wasn't much humor in it. "Yeah," he said, "I want to ask, but I probably don't want you to answer." He reached to ruffle her hair. "Sorry." He looked down at the sloppily iced cinnamon rolls. "Are these to eat or did you just set them there for temptation's sake?"

"You can have *one*," she said. "I don't know how your cholesterol and triglycerides look like these days, but I don't want to be responsible for sending them through the roof."

"Who's going to eat the rest of them?" He looked over the pastries and honed in on the biggest one.

"Your dad gets one, Mother gets one, I get one, and I'll take the rest down to the shop."

"You love the shop, don't you?" He took small bites.

"I do. And not just for myself. Do you know that Mother's working there more hours every week? A lot of times, she'll get busy and before you know it, she's forgetting to use her cane. She won't let me pay her—says that's how she pays her rent here. A couple of the women even asked her to give a class on colors and she's going to do it."

"How's the girl doing who comes in every morning but doesn't talk to anyone?"

"Angie?" Early shook her head. "She still comes in. Since it's gotten colder, anyone driving anywhere near Stringtown stops to pick her up, but she's pretty wise to that—she comes into the store and dusts everything in the place to pay for her ride."

"Why don't you hire her? You could use the help."

"Only through the holidays. And I worry about interfering. I told her once that if she ever needed a place for her and the kids to stay, she should come here. She didn't come in for a week after that. I think I scare her, though I don't know how."

"It's your confidence." Francie came into the kitchen, already dressed in the smock she wore in the shop. She poured coffee, then a glass of water, and stood at the sink to swallow her morning allotment of pills from the plastic container in the drawer. "She knows you wouldn't understand about abuse because you'd never stand for it." She went around the counter to sit beside Nash.

Early frowned. "Well, I don't think I would, though I've never had to *know* because it was never a factor, but I don't see that as a bad thing." She put a roll on a plate and handed it to her mother.

"It's not a bad thing, and I wish I could take the credit for being a good example, but I can't," said Francie. "I'm just telling you why you scare Angie some, is all."

Early stopped in the middle of covering the rest of the rolls to stare at Francie. "Was Dad abusive? I don't remember that."

"Because you weren't around when it happened, and I never told anybody, though some people knew anyhow."

Early thought of Mr. Wilkins and his reserve with her father.

"Mary Brad's parents. They knew, didn't they?"

"Yes. Brad got between us once." Francie picked up the rolls. "I'll go ahead and open up. You won't need to come down before noon unless you see the parking lot filling up. Patty Waylon's coming in to choose some colors for her Sunbonnet Sue quilt. She'll help out if it gets busy."

Francie left the house without her cane, walking with scarcely a limp across the yard to the quilt shop.

"Think she's matchmaking?" asked Nash.

"No, I think she didn't want to talk about it." Early smiled at Ben when he came into the kitchen. "Morning, handsome."

"Hey, sugar." He went to the sink, taking his pill container out of the drawer. He stopped to sniff the air. "Cinnamon rolls?"

"Yours went to the shop with Mother," Early said, "but don't feel too bad. Mine did, too. Oatmeal?"

"I reckon, but the roll would be better." He got a cup of coffee and sat down. "I'm going on a Habitat build in January," he said. "In Arizona."

Early braced herself. She'd known he was going sometime after the holidays and that his doctor had given him a qualified go-ahead, but she was pretty sure Nash hadn't been aware of his father's plans.

He hadn't.

"Dad, you can't! It's only been six months since you had a quintuple bypass!"

"And your cardiologist friend who did that procedure said I could go." Ben went to the refrigerator. "Anyone want some juice?" He took the carton out. "Probably not, because icing would make the juice taste bitter. Since I didn't get any icing, I won't have that problem."

Nash ignored that. "She really said you could go, huh? You got any problem with me talking to her about it?"

His father looked at him, one eyebrow raised in a way that made them look uncannily alike. "Nope. From the looks of you, you need to be talking to her anyway. I don't have the only iffy heart in the family, you know."

Early looked away from Ben, her gaze sharp on Nash's face. "So it's not just me. You *do* look a whole lot like warmed over death." Panic and nausea roiled under her ribs and she was glad she hadn't eaten a cinnamon roll. There was no way it would have stayed down.

"Nicely put," Nash said dryly. "I've got an appointment with her on Monday. No real cause for concern—my numbers don't look that bad at all—but I am going to take some time off. Maybe I'll go to Arizona with you, Dad."

Ben's response was instant. "You'd be welcome. As I remember, you're not that bad of a drywall hanger."

"Fine, then. I'll go. You want to ask Joe?"

Early looked at him again, almost dropping the spoonful of oatmeal she was slapping into a bowl for Ben. "You're willing to spend a week with your brother?"

"Yeah, I am." Nash looked a little surprised himself. "Sometimes when I watch Evan and Logan together, I regret that Joe and I never had that kind of thing, whatever it is. So maybe it's not too late."

She smiled at him and he smiled back.

Ben looked inordinately pleased.

"WHAT DO YOU WANT TO GIVE THE KIDS FOR CHRISTMAS?" NASH walked through the cemetery with Early, his arms loaded with Christmas wreaths.

It was something they'd always decided together; rather, Early decided and gave him half the credit. This year, on his own, Nash was as clueless as he always was. Truthfully, he wished Early would just buy whatever she thought was a good idea and then present him with a bill. That would certainly be easier. For one of them, at least.

She placed a large arrangement of holly and pine cone things on Rosie's grave. "I hadn't even considered it. What do you think?"

So much for her having a good idea.

"They don't want anything." He gave her a hand up from her kneeling position and they walked toward Susan's grave. "I asked."

"Maybe you asked the wrong question."

"Huh?"

"Did you ask the boys if they wanted to go to Arizona with you and Ben and Joe? Or, for that matter, the girls?"

"We're talking about Christmas. And I didn't even know about Arizona when I asked them what they wanted."

"I'm talking about something from their dad."

"In that case," he said, "maybe some time?"

She smiled at him, that open and loving expression he'd taken for granted most of his life. "Good choice, doctor."

He stepped through the gate of Susan's Garden. "Hey, sis." He knelt to help Early spread a grave blanket. "That girl of ours gave us some news. You'd sure be happy." He spoke to Susan as easily as Early did. "What do you think of taking them all on vacation, Susie? Think we can get your little sister to go?" He looked up at his ex-wife. "Would you, Early?"

She sat on the park bench the boys had placed in the garden when their mother's knees started bothering her and gazed at him with troubled eyes. "I think it's probably too late for that," she said quietly. "Don't you?"

No, he didn't think so, or he wouldn't have asked. "We're not married anymore," he admitted, "but we still have a relationship."

"No, we still have a friendship."

"HE LIVES IN THE ASSISTED-LIVING PORTION OF THE NURSING home at the edge of Pleasant Hill. It's named Pleasant Acres, but one of the residents said they all refer to it as Last Call." Joe laid the brown envelope between them on the cutting table in the shop. "I went over there today while you were at the cemetery. Not to talk to him, but to see what he was like. At the time of the lawsuit, he was a sorry-for-himself drunk, and that was the last I knew of him."

"And now?" Early stared at the envelope, wishing she could take it into the living room of the house and toss it into the fire-place. Ben had gotten a nice fire going and he and Francie and a couple of their friends were playing dominoes in front of it. But they'd probably think it odd if she came in and threw a manila envelope into the flames.

Joe hesitated. "I don't know. I saw him from a distance, sitting at the table in the dining room. He still looked the same. The director at the complex said he keeps pretty much to himself. He goes to events, but even then he's alone. No one visits him. I guess Kyle was the last of his family—at least she didn't know about anyone else."

Nash shook his head. "Sarah will want to rescue him."

"We can't tell her before Christmas," said Joe. "She'll invite him for dinner."

They laughed, but Early knew it wasn't really funny; it could very well be the truth. The family worried about Sarah every school year because she became so heavily invested in her students that she was exhausted by Christmas.

"She's a rescuer." Nash's gaze met Early's. "She brings out the best in all of us—remember when Evan spent the afternoon teaching the kids in her class to fish? He doesn't even particularly *like* to fish. Maybe the same will happen with Lambert. He might see what a miracle she is and be a positive force in her life."

His brother gave him a sour look. "Didn't Dad and Mama ever explain to you about Santa and the Easter Bunny?"

Early spread fabric from the ends of bolts, cutting it into fat quarters for the sale basket. She sighed, waiting for the brotherly explosion sure to come.

"Well, yeah," Nash said finally, folding the lengths of calico into neat squares, "but I was in college at the time and I knew they were just kidding." He held up six of the pieces of cloth, fanning them out. "Look, Early, these go together. Did you know that?"

She laughed, relieved that peace would reign for at least a few minutes. "I'd better know that, or I could be out of business."

"They're like the family, I guess." He laid down the six pieces, then got a few more out of the basket and put them with them. "None of them are alike, but they all go together."

Early tossed another swatch on top of the color wheel he'd created, and the incongruity was so instant and startling that the men blinked.

"It only takes one piece to throw the whole combination off." She met Nash's eyes. "Do we have to tell her?"

IN CHURCH THE NEXT MORNING, WITH HIS SISTERS PRESENT, JOHN David announced his engagement to the pretty redhead sitting with her assorted and sundry family in the fourth and fifth pews on the left. As he spoke, Fiona broke free from her mother and walked up the aisle, holding up her arms for the young minister to pick her up. He did, and preached a sermon from Isaiah with a toddler on his hip beaming at the congregation.

Early met Nash's eyes across the family members who were between them. They shared a smile that said each of them knew what the other one was thinking. Not that they could have put it into words—they just knew.

Back at the shop, still in the dress and heels she'd worn to church and then to lunch in Stringtown Proper, Early looked at the fat quarters fanned out on the cutting table. She took the jarring cut of cotton away from the pile and added another one that was as different from the main selection as the first one. Instead of clashing, however, this one added light and energy to the wheel of cloth.

This one was John David.

Thank You, Lord.

Nash looked at the assortment of fabric, then into her eyes. He answered the question she'd asked the night before. "Yeah, we do have to tell her. It's part of Susie's story, and Sarah's entitled to know it."

"I wish I'd never said anything."

"It was going to happen sometime," he said. "Sarah will have children of her own, and she'll want to know if there's anything in her physical background to say she shouldn't. It's better that we help her than if we stood in her way, even though it doesn't feel very good now."

Francie came into the store, turning the sign to declare that A Soft Place to Fall was open for business. She went into the office to hang up her coat, then came out again, checking the pockets of her smock for a pen and reading glasses. "It will be busy in here this afternoon, with just two weeks till Christmas. The girls want to know if you want them to stay and help. You won't want to be working in those high heels, either, Earline. You'll take a tumble and then where will you be?"

Early laughed. She figured she might as well. "I'll still be fifteen pounds overweight and frumpy, Mother, and still trying to find my way to the other side of the road."

CHAPTER 14

NASH LEFT THE CARDIOLOGIST'S BUILDING AND WALKED TOWARD his own, even though he didn't have appointments until two o'clock. He was hungry but didn't feel like eating alone, and it was too late to see if anyone wanted to join him. That was one of the elements of being single he didn't like; when there was no one at home to eat with, chances were good he'd fix a bologna and cheese sandwich or stand at the refrigerator door and eat cold pizza.

The day was cold and bright. Most of the snow that had fallen over the weekend was gone, at least in the city. There had been a thick white coat over the Ridge when he'd driven back this morning, but it had dissipated as he neared Lexington.

It was funny, he thought, that as much as he loved Lexington and always had, his homesickness for the Ridge had taken on a sharp edge since he and Early divorced. Part of the reason was he missed her—he didn't have a problem admitting that—but he didn't know what the rest of it was. He got to see the kids more than their mother did, and he could see a movie, play, or concert without leaving the city limits. He was even starting to get along with his brother.

"Hey!"

He turned. Joe, his coat flapping, was jogging to catch up with him.

"I talked to Early. She wanted to remind you to call her after you left the doctor's office. Said your cell phone was off." He gestured at the pocket of Nash's jacket. "Which it is. I tried to call you, too."

"Nothing ticks me off more than having someone on their cell phone during an appointment, so I turn mine off if I have one. Early knows that." Nash frowned at him. "It's almost noon on a Monday. Shouldn't you be at your office fleecing people? Or having lunch with a client who's intent on fleecing people?"

"Actually, I thought I'd have lunch with you. I'll even buy."

Nash hiked a suspicious eyebrow. "Did the cardiologist call and tell you I was dying or something?"

"Nope. Besides, I've already made out your will, so there's no money to be made from you either way."

"Right." Nash took his phone out of his pocket. "I'm calling Early. You can listen and save me explaining it twice."

"Well, come in here." Joe turned him toward the restaurant on the corner and pulled him through the door. "I can listen better with coffee and a BLT. She's at the shop," he added, when Nash held the phone away from his ear and frowned at it.

"Oh." Irritated because his brother remembered where Early was during the day and he had not, Nash scowled at him again and pushed the memory code for A Soft Place to Fall. "Hi, Francie. Is Early there?"

He had to wait a full minute, forcing himself not to look at his watch. If the truth were told, she had probably cooked entire meals while she waited from him to come to the phone, so maybe it would behoove him to be a little patient. He followed Joe through the nearly empty dining room to a booth in front of a window overlooking a city park. Male cardinals rushed through the trees, and the flashes of color made him ache for the Ridge.

And for something else. He remembered the peace he'd felt standing in the little church at the Corners. He'd thought it was because his family was there, but it was more than that. It was that God was there. Nash wanted that peace again. And he wanted the Lord to be foremost in his heart. But was it too late?

Early's voice finally came, bright and breathless. "Nash? Sorry, it's busy here today. What did she say?"

He smiled, knowing she'd hear it in his voice and breathe a little sigh of relief that she didn't want him to hear. "That I didn't have a heart."

"I *knew* that. Is she going to give you one?"

"Yup. A used model with three new bypasses in it. She found it lying around in my chest not doing anything."

"Oh, Nash."

He closed his eyes for a moment. When he opened them, a cup of coffee steamed in front of him. He met Joe's eyes, the same blue their mother's had been, and read concern there.

"When?"

For a moment, Nash was confused. Who had spoken, Joe or Early? Then he realized they both had, and laughed aloud. "This is a conference call," he said. "Joe's here, too." He sipped the coffee. *Ambrosia. Would he have to give up caffeine altogether? Early made decaf so good he could scarcely tell the difference, but no one else did.*

I need you, Early.

"When?" she repeated.

He sighed. "Friday. I wanted to wait till after the holidays, but she had a cancellation this week and seemed pretty determined to fill the time—I think she's got a kid in college and needs the money. I won't be able to go on the Habitat build with Dad, so it's going to be up to Joe to look after him."

He held out the phone so his brother could hear the expected response. "And who's going to look after Joe?"

Joe grinned and took the phone. "That was hurtful, Early." He listened in silence. "I promise. I'll see you then. Here he is."

"Hey." Nash took his phone back. "I'll be fine. Do you want to tell Dad, though? I know he's worried."

"I'll tell him. What time's your surgery?"

"Nine." He waited for her to say she'd be there. Sitting in the lounge as she had six months ago when Ben was in the OR. She'd be the first person he saw when he woke after surgery. And he wouldn't argue the point; he *wanted* her there.

"You'll have Evan call me?"

The sensation was so quick he didn't know whether it was disappointment or pain, but he had to swallow twice before he said, "You bet."

"I have to go." She sounded breathless again. "I'll call you tonight, okay?"

"Sure." He nodded even though she couldn't see him. "If I'm gone, just leave a message." He put the phone back into his pocket.

A look out the window showed him the cardinals were gone. The park, even with the patches of snow that remained, looked dark and colorless. *Was I right, Lord? Is it too late, both with You and with Early?*

"Friday?" said Joe. "That's quick."

"It is." He was going to have to see about some care when he went home, Nash thought. Maybe the convalescent facility Ben had used before they moved him down to Early's. Panic stirred under his breastbone. "I'm not so sure I shouldn't postpone it. There's not much time to make arrangements."

"Don't do that. There's time."

No, there wasn't. That was a mistake most everybody made, though, thinking there was plenty of time for everything. He remembered missing the kids' events at school and thinking he'd make the next one, but he usually didn't. Before he knew it, Sarah was graduating and it was too late. *Too late.*

When Early had stayed on the Ridge so she could take care of Rosie, she'd urged him to drive down as often as he could to see his mother, because there weren't that many opportunities left. He'd gone, but not often enough. Never often enough.

He'd always thought Early would be there when and where he needed her. Even though he'd made the unilateral choice not to be married anymore, he cherished their friendship, the way they were parents and grandparents together even if they weren't husband and wife. The weekend on the Ridge had been the best he'd had in months.

He'd assumed his ex-wife would be there when he came out of surgery, that she'd invite him to spend time on the Ridge while he recuperated.

The waitress brought their lunch and refills for their coffee, and Nash tried to turn his attention to the food. One thought kept running through is mind, though, and he couldn't seem to stop it.

The woman he hadn't wanted to share his life with had gone out and made one of her own, and there was only room for him along the outer edges.

He knew beyond all doubt that if he asked, she would welcome him into her home to recuperate. She'd run herself ragged between the house and the shop making sure he took his meds, did his exercises, and watched his diet.

While it was true that she was a born nurturer and had spent most of her life being a caregiver to her sister, their kids, and their parents, he wasn't about to add himself to that list. For the first time in her life, she was enjoying at least a modicum of freedom to do what *she* wanted. He wasn't going to get in her way.

It was too late.

∾

"Do you want to go to the hospital when Nash has surgery?" Early looked at Ben across the table at dinner. "I can take you if you do."

"No, there's nothing I can do there." Her father-in-law's gaze held hers for a moment before he passed the steamed vegetables to Francie. "What about you, sugar? Are you going?"

"That's not a good day for me to leave the shop if I don't actually have to." Early picked her way around the carrots on her plate. "The kids will be there." *And Sophie Donato. She's taking his patients while he's off. She'll be there, too.*

"Mary Brad and I can handle the shop, plus I'm sure Angie will be in if you want to go to Lexington." Francie buttered a roll and moved the butter dish out of Ben's reach. "I've been thinking."

Early almost groaned. She had too much on her mind to add more. If Francie was thinking, that was almost never good for her daughter.

But her mother surprised her. "It's time for me to go home. I may be a little afraid to—there's no getting around that—but I don't think that's going to go away. I can still come and work in the shop as much as I do now, plus it will be good for me to keep my own house again. I raised you up telling you the Lord helped them that helped themselves. It's time I was one of them."

"Are you sure?" Early said with a little apology heavenward for her uncharitable thoughts.

"I'm sure. I can pick up Angie on the road each morning and it will be legitimate that I'm going that way. We won't have to think up errands anymore as excuses to give her a ride, leastways on the days I work." Francie sounded decisive, and her expression was closer to happy than Early thought she'd ever seen it. "I thought maybe I could offer to pay her some for doing the heavy work in the house. It might help her financially plus give her a boost in that self-esteem everyone's always talking about these days."

"That sounds like a great idea." Early went around the table to give her mother a hug. "Just let me know if it doesn't work out."

"Okay." Francie squeezed back, just for an instant, then gave her a little push. "Enough of your foolishness. Ben and I need to get over to the senior center for the dominoes tournament. The winners get gift certificates at that new restaurant."

When they left, Early started the dishwasher and put on a coat to walk down to the shop. She had plenty of commissioned projects to be completed on the long-arm quilting machine, and she usually did them after the shop closed because the machine was noisy. But tonight she wanted quiet.

She brewed a pot of tea and sat at the quilt frame in Rosie's Corner, reaching for one of the threaded needles that was always at the ready. The quilt on the frame was a double wedding ring, pieced years ago by Rosie in the vibrant colors Sarah loved. It would be Sarah and John David's gift from a loving grandmother. Early stitched fast and straight, her fingers rocking the tiny needle through the sandwich of fabric and batting. She loved all kinds of sewing, but hand-stitching was the most relaxing, giving ease to her frenetic thoughts.

Compartmentalizing in the way Nash had mastered and she was working on—really, she was—she put concerns about Sarah on her mind's back burner.

She would think about the shop, Early decided, tying a quilter's knot and reaching for another needle. The batiks she'd received from a new wholesaler were sub-standard and would have to be sent back. She'd been so worried about having too much holiday fabric on hand that she wasn't sure she had enough. She and the other quilt shop owners or managers on or near the Ridge were planning a shop-hop promotion in February and she wasn't sure how she was going to find the time. She had to get material prepared for the class due to start in January.

That thought process kept her busy through three lengths of thread and one cup of tea. When she got up to refill her cup, her gaze fell on the table holding the basket of fat quarters. She'd fanned the ones Nash had chosen into a display in front of the old wicker container, complete with thread, a fat pin cushion, and a pair of wire-framed reading glasses.

Someone had bought the entire selection this morning. The area where it had been was bare; no one had found the time to put anything else in its place.

Early started to move the basket to the center of the table so the empty space on the white table cover wouldn't be so obvious, but she changed her mind and left it where it was. Because no matter how hard you tried, some spaces just couldn't be filled.

"ARE YOU GOING TO OBSERVE?" IF NASH WERE A LITTLE MORE medicated and didn't have his glasses on, looking up at his oldest son would be like looking into the mirror.

Evan shook his head. "Nope. There are limits to how much I can distance myself."

His father was glad to hear that. While he was the first to admit he often had trouble separating the patient from the disease, sometimes he feared Evan was *too* good at it.

"You'll call your mother and your grandparents?"

"Uh-huh."

"Time to go nighty-night, Dr. Nash." A nurse came into the pre-op cubicle. "Have you seen everybody you need to?"

No. "Yeah. Let's get going before the surgeon leaves for breakfast."

There was a rustling sound, and someone else stepped around Evan.

"I couldn't do it." Early wasn't wearing makeup and her hair was barely combed. She looked wonderful. "I had to come in and make sure you hadn't changed your will just because we got a divorce."

He lifted his hand—which took real effort; the medication must be working—and she laid hers in it. "Too late, but I still left you my widescreen TV and my recliner to keep your next fella comfortable."

She laughed, though it caught in her throat, and squeezed his hand. "Then you better get well fast, or they'll find themselves in the Goodwill store." She bent to kiss his cheek, lifting his glasses away from his face when she straightened. "I'll see you when you wake up."

"Thanks for coming." He hoped he smiled at her. He meant to. But he was so sleepy. "Evan?"

"I'm here."

"Take care of your mother."

"We will." His son's hand brushed his face where Early's lips had.

"Love you, Dad."

"Careful, Nash. He's sucking up." She took his hand again when the nursing staff had maneuvered him into the hallway, and held it until they reached the double doors that led into the surgery suite. "See you soon," she promised.

Okay. He could live with that.

THE COFFEE IN THE SURGERY WAITING ROOM WAS FRESH, JUST AS it had been when Early waited for news about Ben. After a side trip into a restroom to brush her hair and put on enough makeup that her reflection no longer frightened her, she filled her commuter cup and stood at the window, looking out at the gray day. The children had gone back to work at Nash's behest after setting up a rapid dissemination calling order. "Mama can call Evan and Grandpa, then Evan can call Logan, who can call Anna…" Jessie's voice had faded away as they went down the corridor toward the bank of elevators at its end.

Early wondered if they would have stayed in the waiting room if she hadn't shown up. The relief on their faces when she'd stepped off the elevator would have been comical if they hadn't all been so concerned about Nash. They'd all hugged her.

"He'll be safe now. You'll take care of him." Jessie had whispered.

She bowed her head, praying silently and fervently for help in doing just that. *Keep him safe, Lord, in the palm of Your hand. I will say, Not my will but Thine be done. Help me to mean it.*

Opening her eyes, she stared out the window of the waiting room, thinking of other times she'd been here. "Here I am again."

She said the words aloud, but didn't expect an answer in the deserted room, so she was surprised and embarrassed to feel someone's presence right in front of her. Even more surprised when the presence spoke in a voice filled to overflowing with both disdain and challenge.

"Again or still? You never really left, did you?"

Early's first inclination was to get up and walk out without responding, but she reconsidered that before she even set her cup down. She didn't owe Sophie Donato a thing. Including leaving.

"No, I wasn't the one who left." She wasn't certain what protocol was for ex-wives in surgery waiting rooms, but she was pretty sure best friends were welcome.

"Don't you think it's time to step aside?"

"Aside from what? Nash and I are divorced. That's as far as I'm stepping. We still share children and grandchildren and the community where we grew up. We're also still friends. I'm sorry if you have a problem with that." *No, I'm not. I really don't* care *if you have a problem with that.*

"Your children are *grown*, Earline. It's not necessary to involve Nash in every facet of their lives. He lives in Lexington, not on your precious Ridge. And if he needs a friend, I'm here. He doesn't need you."

Early's insides churned. Mary Brad had once told her she didn't have a nasty bone in her body. It was time she found one. "I think we'll leave that decision up to him. He's a big boy. What do you say?"

Sophie crossed her arms tightly in front of her, reminding Early forcibly of the doctor's superiority in more than one area. "Not good enough. He's never going to go on with his life if you don't stay out of it. Stop playing the martyr and let his father go to a nursing home if he can't take care of himself anymore, for goodness' sake. Nash and his brother will both be more available if the old man's here in Lexington than if he's halfway to Tennessee." She smiled, the expression both brilliant and false. "And you *won't* be available. What could be better?"

"My goodness, you do have ideas, don't you?" Early hadn't known it was possible to even speak when rage was boiling up inside like a geyser. But it was. Not only possible but necessary. "Have you discussed this with Nash and Joe? Or with Ben? It's amazing, but he's fully able to decide for himself where he wants to live. I've never heard him mention a nursing home, but I suppose anything could happen." She picked her cup up again, lifting it to her lips. Her hand was shaking and the plastic cup clacked against her teeth.

"Nash's father really isn't my concern."

"I'd just about figured that out for myself." Early sipped again, soothed by the fragrant brew. "However, he is mine, and he'll stay on the Ridge as long as he likes. If you're not satisfied with that, I suggest you take it up with Nash."

"I might just do that."

Early had thought she only disliked Sophie because the beautiful doctor was involved with Nash. She had given herself long, silent lectures about being civil to her and had urged the children to do likewise. She'd prayed for forbearance, had looked for things to like in the other woman. After all, Sophie hadn't wrecked their home. Nash had.

But it went deeper than that.

"You remind me of Reginald."

Sophie's eyes widened. "Who?"

"Reginald. He's a pedigreed rooster who belongs to my friend Mary Brad. He's gorgeous, very expensive, and rules the henhouse with an iron…claw. But the hens hate him. They're in a constant state of upset, pecking each other and pulling feathers out, not laying eggs, not eating. I think it's because it's all about him. He really doesn't care about the hens or anything else. You're that way. You're beautiful, no doubt about that, and you must be a good doctor or Jason and Nash wouldn't have you as an interim in the practice. I suppose at some level, you might care about Nash. In the end, though, it's all about you, isn't it?"

Sophie expelled a long, hissing breath. "Righteous, aren't you?"

Early shrugged, getting to her feet. "Maybe. But, whatever I am, I am here because my best friend and my kids' father is having surgery, and I'm worried about him. So, get out of my face, Sophie. And stay out."

Ignoring the other woman's look of outrage, Early walked away and sat on the love seat near the window, opening the paperback she'd brought with her.

What if Nash marries her? The very thought of it made her stomach roil. She would never see Nash again other than at weddings and funerals. If the truth were told, she wouldn't blame Sophie for not wanting the old wife hanging around getting in the way. In her head, anyway; her heart would blame her forever.

Sometimes being the old wife really did suck.

The blinking Christmas tree in the corner of the waiting room caught her attention and she laid her book aside as she looked back. They'd spent last year's holidays in the house on Canterbury Crossing. Nash and Evan were on call for Thanksgiving, so they both had Christmas uninterrupted at home. It was as noisy and glorious as it always was. Early had been happy, cooking and playing with grandchildren and carrying on three conversations at once.

Reluctantly, she remembered last Christmas Eve, too, when Nash looked over at her in bed and said, "Maybe next year, we could take that cruise we've always talked about. Over the holidays, I mean. Celebrate with the kids and then get on a plane. What do you say?"

She hadn't really said anything at all. Just a tentative, "I don't know. We'll have to see."

But she hadn't meant it. The holidays *were* the kids to her. She and Nash could go on a cruise any time he deigned to take time off and go. There would be only so many Christmas mornings to wake up with toddlers bouncing on their bed, so many Christmas nights with all four children in the house.

She'd always accused Nash of not listening. "You sit in your recliner in front of the TV and say 'uh-huh' at all the right times. That is not an adult way to carry on a conversation."

Listening only when you liked what the other person was saying wasn't too adult, either. Was that the difference between wives and girlfriends? Did Sophie listen closely when Nash spoke of world travel and playing every golf course on the Robert Trent Jones Trail?

Early didn't even have a passport. Her idea of world travel

was watching Rick Steves specials on educational channels. She didn't care where Nash or anyone else played golf.

Regret drew a sharp edge in her heart. If she had it to do over again, she thought she'd go on a holiday cruise with her husband. At least once.

CHAPTER 15

NASH HAD BEEN A PATIENT BEFORE. HE DIDN'T LIKE IT. AND HE wasn't good at it. Janine Cramer, who'd graduated from nursing school when he was ten years old, glowered at him as she took his vitals. "Now, look here, useless, they're going to start referring to you as Dr. Nasty instead of Dr. Adorable if you don't straighten up."

"I thought it was Dr. Darlin'."

"That's Evan. I swear, I don't know how Early put up with you as long as she did."

"It was a lapse in judgment, I'm sure. Not unlike the fact that Tom has stayed married to you for at least a hundred years."

"It's my gentle touch and winning personality."

He wasn't going to go near that line, especially since she did have a remarkably tender touch and both he and Tom Cramer liked her personality just fine the way it was. "When's breakfast?"

"When it gets here. When are you going home?"

"As soon as I can. A man can't get better in a hospital."

"Where are you going? Over to that convalescent place where your dad was?"

"Home. The kids and Joe will be in and out, and I've hired Home Health Care for a few weeks."

"Dr. Donato will be close by, too, I reckon."

The nurse's voice was so stiff, Nash nearly grinned. Many of the nursing staff disliked Sophie, but they were uniform in their fondness for Early. He wondered if the ex-Mrs. Dr. McGrath had any idea of the size and loyalty of her fan club.

"Sophie's all right," he said, "and she's a fine physician, but probably not the convalescent-care type. Where are my glasses, by the way? I can only read the bold print in the newspaper without them."

"They're here." Janine handed him the case from the bedside table. "Early ran them over to the optometrist's office and had them straightened and tightened up some yesterday while you were sleeping."

He remembered his first few years in private practice, when he'd been an associate in a family health clinic. He'd been the low man, working weekends and being on call more than the other three doctors. Even though he'd loved the work, he'd been largely *in absentia* at home. Coming into the house at three o'clock one morning, he'd found his wife ironing the white shirts and lab coats he wore every day.

"Don't you usually send these out?" He ran a finger along the blade-sharp sleeve crease.

"They don't do them right." She smiled at him. "My part of being the doctor's wife, now that I no longer hawk Quarter Pounders and fries, is being sure you wear neat clothes."

"But why do them now?" He gestured at the clock on the kitchen wall.

"Because the only good ironing time is when everyone's asleep."

He made hot chocolate while she finished the last shirt, and they sat together on the lumpy old couch to drink it. "Someday we'll have a big new house and you won't ever have to iron anything ever again." He clicked his cup against hers in a toast.

"What if I want to?"

That had seemed silly then, and they'd laughed at the preposterousness of the notion, but she ironed for him until he started wearing sweaters and a laundry service maintained lab coats for the practice.

Nash took his glasses out of the case. They weren't smudged, or crooked, or so loose one of the temple pieces was in danger of falling off. Why hadn't he taken care of that himself? *Before* the frame nearly went to pieces.

"Come and see your mother!" Early had shouted over the phone during those months of Rosie's last illness. *"It's going to be too late!"*

Too late was becoming the story of his life.

Forgive me, Lord. Forgive me.

"YOU KNOW WHAT? THIS IS WHAT WE DID WHEN YOUR grandparents got sick. It's what they do in movies when they're building up to the climax. The family meets, all gloom and doom, and decides what to do and how to cope." Early looked around the restaurant table at her children. "What kind of stuff is that? Your dad is absolutely able to decide these things for himself."

"But he won't, Mom." Logan refilled his coffee cup and passed the carafe to his brother.

"He will and he did. He's going home this afternoon and Home Health Care will come twice a day. One of you will come every day, too, or at least call. Joe will check when he gets home at night. Your dad's meals will be delivered for the first two weeks by Off Your Feed, that company that caters to homebound convalescents. I'll call him. So will your grandfather and Granny

Fran. He'll be fine." Early met their eyes in turn. "Sophie will be around." The words sounded stiff in spite of herself.

"He would be better if he went home with you." Sarah said what her mother was certain they were all thinking. "We would, too."

"I know you would, honey."

Early was going to give in. They knew it and she knew it. She wasn't even sure why she was putting up this pseudo-battle against it. It reminded her of when they were teenagers. When Nash said, "We'll see," in response to a request, they knew it meant, "Probably not." When their mother said, "We'll see," they got their coats; they knew it meant, "Yes."

When she'd gotten home from Lexington on the day of Nash's surgery, her mother's room had been emptied of all Francie's possessions, the rented hospital bed made with fresh sheets and a new pillow from the linen closet. White towels—Francie always used colored ones—hung in the bathroom. The wireless call bell lay on the bedside table.

Francie was still in the shop. It was closed, but she was restocking shelves and arranging displays.

"Everyone helped with my things. Angie carried everything into the house for me," she said. "It's time for me to go home, and I'm excited about it." Her eyes, the same blue as Susan and Sarah's, shimmered for a moment. "No one could ask for a better daughter than you, Earline. I am so grateful. But if Nash needs a place to stay, it needs to be ready for him."

Three days later, Early sat at a restaurant with her children while they asked her to take their father home with her.

"It would probably just be for a couple of weeks, Mom," said Evan. He exchanged a glance with his brother and sisters. "We do understand what we're asking of you. We know it's not fair."

"All right." Early held up her hands to forestall further pleas. "I'll ask him. If he says no, we're stopping there."

Forty-five minutes later, that's exactly what he said. "And we're not going to argue about it, either." He was dressed in a workout suit and tennis shoes, ready to leave the hospital.

He looked awful.

"Daddy, we don't want you to be alone." Sarah, who had come to the hospital with Early, knelt beside his chair.

"You kids can check in every day. So can your mother, if she wants to, but she's not going to spend her days running between the shop and a convalescent ex-husband Janine Cramer calls 'useless' in a gesture I'm determined is affection."

Evan laughed. "And she's in a position to know." He looked at his watch and tugged at his sister's arm. "I need to get back to the office and you've got about seven minutes before you have to be standing in your classroom looking like a schoolteacher. Dad, whatever you decide to do, let us know."

"I will."

When they had gone, Early sat on the edge of the bed and looked at Nash. "Are you sure?"

"I'm not sure about anything," he admitted. "I always thought I'd accepted mortality pretty well—except for children, I mean— but it's different when it's your own life you're thinking about. There are all these regrets. This sense of being too late."

"But it's not." She bent her head to force him to meet her gaze. "It's not too late. You're spending time with the kids, with Joe, with Ben. You got your heart fixed." She straightened, steeling herself. "You're more than welcome to come to the Ridge to recuperate, to figure out how to change the habits that are going to kill you if you let them. We have a support system in place there already. But recovery is up to you. If you choose the recliner, regret, and despair, you're on your own and you're not going to do it on my time."

He laughed, and there was the ghost of the old twinkle in his eyes. "Early, are you trying to talk me *into* coming to the Ridge or *out* of it?"

The truth was that she didn't know. They'd lived apart for eleven months and been divorced for seven. Although he'd spent holidays and sporadic weekends on the Ridge in the months since she moved, they hadn't shared a house, they hadn't been alone. They talked on the phone a couple of times a week and were both part of the family email and text list. She missed him every single day and thought she always would.

But.

"Out of it." She smiled at him, although she didn't feel like it at all. "I'm not much of a nurse. But I do worry about you being alone."

"I'll be fine." He gave her hand a squeeze. "Promise. And you know my promises are good for thirty years or so. After that, all bets are off."

Early turned off the radio as she drove back to the Ridge and called her father-in-law to tell him Nash wouldn't be coming back with her.

When she got home, she checked on the status of the shop. "Just take the afternoon off," Mary Brad suggested, waving her away after hearing the report on Nash's welfare. "We'll call you if it gets crazy later on."

In the house, Ben was packing.

"I thought the build wasn't till next month." She stood in the door of his room, thinking how much better he looked than he had six months before.

"It's not. I'm going to go up and spend a week or two with Nash. We should have thought of it before. I'm plenty capable of seeing he takes his meds and doesn't overdo anything."

For a moment, she was too startled to speak. "Of course, you are." *But who will take care of you? It's not just Nash and Joe who need looking after.* "Why don't you wait till tomorrow? It will be dark before you get there."

He grinned at her, that emotionally lethal expression that seemed exclusive to McGrath men, and she knew he'd read her thoughts as well as hearing what she said. "Don't worry. We'll all be here for Christmas."

While he finished packing, she filled a cooler with single servings of food from the freezer in the garage. "Get Joe to carry this stuff in for you." She set the cooler in the trunk of Ben's car beside his suitcase, knowing full well he'd probably carry them both into the apartment building by himself. "It's just stuff I've cooked for you and Mother to eat when I wasn't here. Nash complains about healthy stuff, but he'll eat it if someone fixes it for him."

"All right." Ben gave her a hug and kissed her cheek. "Enjoy the quiet time, sugar. I'll be home soon enough."

She nodded. "Just be careful."

After waving him off, she tossed Ben's sheets into the washer and started it, then poured a cup of coffee. She took it into the sewing room, plugged in the Christmas tree, and settled into the corner of the love seat with a blanket over her feet to watch darkness descend over the Ridge.

It's a Wonderful Life was in the DVD player, and she started the old movie at its beginning, figuring she'd be asleep by the time George Bailey married Mary Hatch and they became a perfect couple. "That's us," Nash used to say, pointing at James Stewart and Donna Reed, portraying George and Mary, "starting out poor and having too many kids."

The phone rang an hour later, waking Early from a fairly deep doze. "Dad's here." Nash's voice sounded stronger than it had earlier today. "Thanks for sending the food."

"You're welcome. How are you feeling?"

"Pretty good, actually, though not up to anything much more difficult than thumbing the remote. How about you?"

What a change that was. In times past, he wouldn't have asked that; he would have taken it for granted she was fine simply because she always was.

"I'm okay. Watching *It's a Wonderful Life.*"

He chuckled. "Me, too."

"Well, enjoy it, then. You and Ben take care of each other."

"We will. Goodnight, Mary Hatch. Sleep warm."

She had to catch her breath before she could speak as though she wasn't crying. She closed her eyes and swallowed hard. Then swallowed again. "You, too, George Bailey."

CHAPTER 16

"I FEEL LIKE NED." MARY BRAD CAST FURTIVE LOOKS LEFT AND right as she walked up the carpeted corridor of Pleasant Acres Assisted Living with Early.

"Who's Ned?"

"You know, Nancy Drew's boyfriend."

Early gave her a sideways look. "You're dressed all wrong, and the makeup wouldn't look good on Ned, either. You're more like Bess."

"Who's Bess?"

"One of Nancy's girlfriends."

"Oh." Mary Brad frowned. "I can't remem…oh, yes, I do. Bess was the plump one, wasn't she? The blonde. I prefer to be the other one. What was her name? George, that's it." She fluffed her hair. "I'm a natural brunette, after all."

Early snorted. "You haven't seen your natural color in so many years, you have no idea what it is."

"Got no intention of finding out, either. There he is."

They stopped walking, as in step as they'd been in their baton-twirling days. Early yelped when a mobility scooter nearly knocked her off her feet.

"Keep moving, girlie," advised its occupant, moving past them at an alarming clip. "It's lunch time in Last Call."

"Sorry." But Early was looking at the man at the end of the hall, making his laborious way toward the central dining room of the facility. "He's huge."

Sarah was so slender her brothers teased her that if she stood sideways and stuck out her tongue, she'd be mistaken for a zipper, but she had a lumberjack's appetite. Nash was that way, too, and they often forgot she couldn't have inherited the tendency from him.

"She doesn't look like him at all. Joe's made a mistake," said Mary Brad decisively. "Let's go home. I'm hungry."

"It wasn't Joe's decision. He looked for every way around it. It was DNA." Early frowned. "But I thought he was in a wheelchair."

"Obviously not all the time, which is too bad. It couldn't happen to a nicer guy. Forgive me, Lord. I didn't mean that. Exactly." Scowling, Mary Brad hefted the bag of lap quilts she was carrying. "Come on, let's get it over with. You sure we brought enough?"

"Should be, unless something's changed in the past couple of days. I called ahead." Early set down her sack of quilts so she could rummage in the tote bag she had on her shoulder. "I have the treat bags here, too. Are you going to be the announcer while I start handing things out? I can get a closer look at him that way."

"Do I look like Santa Claus to you?"

"You would if you let your roots grow out."

"I take back what I said about you growing a nasty bone. I liked you better without it."

"Too late. You led me down the path to nice-girl destruction and now you'll have to pay the price."

"What are you going to say to him? 'Hey, did you rape my

handicapped sister?' probably wouldn't get you anywhere in the information department."

"Speaking of nasty bones…"

Mary Brad tossed a wicked grin over her shoulder and led the way into the dining area. "Good morning! How are you all today? Have you looked outside? I swear it's cold enough out there to freeze a witch's parts. I'm Mary Brad Hardesty and the cranky-looking woman there in the back is my friend Early McGrath. We're glad to meet y'all. I'm sorry to be interrupting your lunch, but the nice lady in the office said it was the best time to catch you together."

The people at the tables gave her polite attention, a couple of them even applauding her cheerleader demeanor.

Encouraged, not to mention being totally irrepressible, she continued. "Early and I don't have any men to keep life interesting for us—"

That little pearl of good-old-boy fodder was met with guffaws from the male contingent in the room, and even the women laughed politely.

"—or for that matter, to keep us so busy running after them that we don't have any time for ourselves, so we like to make quilts. Since it's nearly Christmas, we hope you won't mind taking these particular ones off our hands, because we've run plumb out of shelf space. We have bags of candy for you, too. Not that any of you would eat candy, of course, but it's nice to have when the grandkids come to visit. Keeps them from playing in the toilet while you're trying to talk."

She waved an all-encompassing arm, and Early noticed that her friend still had great muscle tone. That wasn't very loyal of her.

"Early's going to start around that way and I'll go this way. If you want to talk to us, that's fine—we love to talk—but if you just want to go on eating, that's fine, too. We understand you call the facility Last Call—if that means they're going to take your plates away whether you're done or not, you just feel free to ignore us."

Shaking her head and laughing, though her stomach felt as though it might revolt at any second, Early approached the nearest table. "It's Mrs. Redding, isn't it? I think you were my geometry teacher."

"I was." The woman beamed, her eyes as sharp as they'd been over thirty years ago. "I taught that boy you married, too. Francie Winslow was always just so proud of him. He became a doctor, didn't he?"

"He did, a good one." Early drew quilts out of her bag. "You have a preference? This nine-patch looks particularly geometric. Almost blinded me when I quilted it."

The retired teacher laughed and stroked loving hands over the surface of the quilt. "Thank you so much."

The next quilt went to a wizened man who gave her a distrustful look even as he tucked the blanket around his legs. A blind woman sat at the next table. "Just give me an ugly one if you have it," she requested. "It will still feel beautiful to me."

Early dug to the bottom of the bag for what she considered the prettiest quilt she'd brought. "It's a warm one."

"Oh, yes." The woman's hands, age-spotted but still lovely, ran over the fabric. "But it's pretty, too. I can tell."

"So are you." Early took her hand and shook it. "I can tell, too."

Frank Lambert sat in a wheelchair at the fifth table she approached. He shoveled his lasagna in a way that made her think of Clarissa the cat when she'd first come to live with Early. It was as though if he didn't eat everything on his plate as quickly as he could, someone would take it away from him.

"Just leave it there." He pointed with his fork at the empty chair across from him. "The candy, too."

Early had to force her voice to remain even. "Don't I know you from somewhere? Did you grow up around here?"

"Part of the time. We lived in Over Yonder."

"What's your name?"

"Frank Lambert." He didn't look at her, just spoke between bites.

"Don't you have a brother?"

"Did. Kyle. He's dead." His voice was still emotionless, but something flashed in his eyes.

"What happened to him?"

"Mine explosion."

"I lost friends in that."

"I know." He stopped eating long enough to look up at her, his expression indifferent but his gaze cold. "I know who you are, because your noisy friend up there just told us. And I know who you married. Who your worthless brother-in-law is. You haven't been anywhere I was since the explosion. Why now? What do you want?"

What she wanted was for the DNA test to be wrong, but that wasn't going to happen. She kept her voice calm. "My 'worthless brother-in-law' did a good job of protecting your interests."

"Got himself rich in the process, though, didn't he?" His sneer showed that he hadn't spent much of his settlement on dental work.

"Not so much." Early gave blankets and sacks of candy to the occupants of the next table before turning back to Frank Lambert. "Do you remember my sister?"

"The retard?" He bit off half a piece of garlic bread. "Sure, I remember her. Why?"

Early hardly ever got truly angry, and even when she did, she didn't stay that way for long. However, at this moment, as rage flowed over her like the molten lava she'd seen in disaster movies, she was certain she would stay mad at this ugly man for the rest of her natural life. It took her a few seconds, but she got her breathing under control. "You were with her, weren't you?"

"What of it?"

She walked away. Getting arrested for assaulting a morbidly obese man wouldn't be helpful. Satisfying, maybe, but not productive. It wouldn't answer the question of what or how to tell Sarah about her biological father.

Smiling and talking—she never knew how she did it—she handed out the rest of the quilts and candy in her bag, then stood still at the back of the room. Anger still roared like a freight train through her veins. Now that the purpose of giving the gifts had been fulfilled, she didn't know what to do with herself.

"Early, are you ready?" Mary Brad appeared beside her, empty bag in hand. "It looks as though we had enough to go around."

"I'm ready."

As she walked past the table where Frank Lambert sat, she picked up the quilt and sack of candy she'd left there. "Actually," she said, "we had one more than we needed."

"Hey!" Lambert's bellow followed them as they moved toward the front door. "Bring them back."

They kept going, stepping outside and breathing deeply of the crisp, cold air. Early felt lightheaded. Maybe one could live with that kind of anger, but she wasn't sure how.

Mary Brad eyed her across the top of the car. "Let's have lunch before we go back to the shop. I've heard the owner's a soft touch. She won't mind if we're late."

"Especially if you're buying."

"That works."

A Soft Place to Fall was busy that afternoon, giving Early little time to think about either the events of the morning or Nash.

Josh called at six o'clock. "I figured you'd be good and tired by now and your resistance would be down. How about dinner? I have a roast in the oven and not even I can ruin that."

"What can I bring?"

"Just yourself."

"I can't be there before eight. We're staying open a little later this weekend."

"I'll be waiting."

She closed the shop without even running the vacuum cleaner, locking the deposit in the safe in the office and shooing Angie, Mary Brad, and Francie out the door ahead of her. "I can clean and set up in the morning. It's been a long enough day already." She locked the door.

"It has at that." Her mother flapped a wave at them and went to her car. "I'll see you girls in the morning. You get some rest now."

Angie waved in smiling silence before getting into the passenger side of Francie's car.

"Your mother doesn't know you have a date, does she?" Mary Brad mumbled as they stepped off the porch of the shop.

"Are you kidding? She'd have locked me in the house." Early hiked an eyebrow at her friend. "What about you?"

"There's a lawyer I know waiting for me."

"How many times has Joe proposed to you?"

"Four. Once when I was married and Paul told him he didn't have a big enough dowry for us to get divorced. Then he asked every time he got a divorce."

"Are you going to say yes next time?"

Mary Brad blushed. "Who knows if there'll be a next time?"

"There will." Early gave her a hug. "See you in church."

She showered quickly, dressed in black pants and a green sweater with sparkling threads knit into it, put on fresh makeup, and drove to Josh's house. She hadn't seen him since the night they'd talked about Susan, though they'd talked on the phone several times, and she felt a little thrill of anticipation. Sort of.

He met her at the door with a kiss and a hug. "I've missed you." He held her gaze. "Are you all right?"

"Sure. Just tired. The quilt shop is doing much better than I anticipated. The price of success is being exhausted." She smiled at him. He was wearing gray slacks and a burgundy sweater. "You look good. School year going well?"

"It is, though I'm tired, too. I keep telling those kids the least they could do, since I share what I know with them, is to share their energy with me. Want some coffee?"

"Sure." She followed him toward his kitchen and accepted the cup he proffered.

He gestured toward the table in the dining area. "Have a seat. I'll bring dinner in."

She sat down, reflecting how odd it felt to be waited on. She thought she should probably offer to help, but doing nothing felt too good to risk his acceptance.

"How did Nash do with his surgery?" He carried bowls of salad in and set them at their places. "Noah said Jessie was worried about him."

"He's doing pretty well. He's going to have to change his life-style, which he's not at all thrilled about, but he'll be fine, I think."

"Does he play golf?"

"Yes. He didn't used to, but the kids all played in high school and college. It was a way to spend time with them, so he got to where he enjoyed it." She'd forgotten that. Not that he played—the time he spent on the golf course used to irritate her—but how he got started. It was amazing the things you could forget when you wanted the other guy to be the bad one.

Josh nodded understanding. "That's how I spent time with Noah. Rebecca hated golf. Still does, I think."

"Are you going to Rebecca's for Christmas?" Noah was coming to Early's house with Jessie, but Early didn't know if Noah's father was aware of that.

"Yes." He smiled, though his eyes were sad. "Noah will be with you, I understand. That's fine with me, but Rebecca's a little harder to convince."

Early nodded. "I remember the first holiday Logan and Anna spent with her family. I nearly went into withdrawal. But then it was Evan, skiing somewhere instead of coming home, and the girls have been away a few times, too. I do love it when everyone comes, though."

Josh hesitated. "Have you found who Sarah's father is? I hate to ask because I know it's not really my business, but I've still got some guilt going on there.".

"Frank Lambert."

"Oh." Josh reached for his water glass and took a healthy swallow. "I'm sorry."

"Me, too." She pushed her salad plate away. "We haven't told her yet."

"Will that be hard?"

"Yes." *Oh, Sarah, please don't be hurt. Please.*

"I remember when we told Rebecca she was adopted. She went off the deep end, and we had a few troublesome years with her. Noah, on the other hand, thought it was cool. Rebecca found her birth parents after Jackie died. It was all right with me. I helped her search and went with her and her husband to meet them. Her birth mother is wise enough not to have tried to take Jackie's place, and they've established a good relationship."

"What about Noah?"

"He never talks about it."

They ate dinner, finishing off the pot of coffee, and loaded the dishwasher, then adjourned to the living room to watch a movie. Josh, the dutiful host, passed over an adventure film in favor of a romantic comedy, then took Early's attention away from the screen by kissing her. "I've missed you."

She smiled. She'd been lonely in the days Ben had been gone. It was good to be with someone.

"WHAT ARE YOU SAYING?" SOPHIE DONATO'S EYES FLASHED, AND Nash wished she'd put down the steak knife she was brandishing.

"That we need to stop seeing each other." He wouldn't duck, he told himself, unless she pointed the knife at him. Which he didn't think she would do. Not seriously, anyway.

"She got to you, didn't she?"

"She who?"

"Don't play dumb with me, Nash. How many 'shes' do you have in your life? I'm talking about your ex-wife. She told you about our conversation, didn't she?"

"What conversation would that be?"

"The one while she was in the surgery waiting room."

"I must have missed that one. I was kind of busy. And, no, Early never mentioned it. Should she have?"

"No, it was private. I just thought she might have." Sophie finally put down the knife and pushed away her plate, leaving her steak half-eaten. "You need to explain to me, though, Nash, why we need to stop seeing each other. It's not as though we've taken a vow of exclusivity or anything. Your freedom hasn't been compromised."

"I know." He wasn't hungry, either, plus he was agonizingly tired. He wished he'd never started this conversation, but it was too late for that. "I've made a few discoveries about myself over the past ten days or so, Soph. One of them is that I'm the monoga-mous type. I need to be loyal to someone. The other is that some-times freedom's overrated."

"So what are you going to do? Reconcile with Early?"

"No." He smiled at Sophie and reached for her hands. It would keep her from picking the knife back up. "For a while, I'm not going to do anything except get myself healthy, spend time with my kids and my dad, and make friends with my brother."

"But what about her?" Sophie was insistent. "I can't help feeling that she's behind this."

"In a way she probably is. We got married so young that we grew up together and in large part, each of us shaped whatever the other one became. I depended on her too much, which made me a demanding cuss who never gave as much as he got. She, on the other hand, spent her whole life taking care of things for people. She's learning to do for herself, now, instead of putting everyone else's wants and needs first every single time. I'm learning not to expect everything from other people and nothing from myself."

"What does that have to do with you and me?"

"Everything." He shook her hands for emphasis. "I like you, Sophie, and I've enjoyed these past months, but whether we like it or not, we're both takers when it comes to relationships. There's nothing wrong with that, I guess, if it's what people want to do, but I don't want to anymore."

"I can't change your mind?"

"No."

They'd met at a restaurant, though Nash had taken a taxi because he wasn't supposed to drive yet. They parted at the door, and he waited with the doorman for another taxi to drive past, not in enough of a hurry to call one. Relief made him feel lighter and healthier, although melancholy lingered somewhere in the back of his mind. It was tempting to walk back to the apartment, but he knew better. He wasn't yet to the six-block-brisk-walk point in his recovery.

"Hey!"

He looked up at the shout, and waved at Evan, who was double-parked across the street.

"I'm going home," his son called. "Want a ride?"

Nash crossed and settled into the passenger seat of Evan's car. "Were you stalking your own father? That's sick, Evan."

"Just left the hospital. I'm on call. I saw Sophie leave. She didn't look all that happy, so I drove around the block to see if you were hoofing it."

"Yeah. I don't think I made her very happy."

They rode for a little while, their silence broken only by Evan's humming. It took a few blocks for Nash to recognize the tune.

"You're too young to know Neil Sedaka songs."

"Not that one, Dad. 'Breaking Up is Hard to Do' is a classic among men. Uncle Joe knows it backwards and forwards."

Nash laughed so hard it made his incision hurt. "Your mother would like that," he said, pulling his phone out of his pocket.

"She isn't home."

"Really?" Nash looked at the dashboard clock. It wasn't late by many standards, but according to Early McGrath's internal clock, it was time for pajamas and hot chocolate.

"Yes, it's already been through the calling grapevine that it's Friday night and Mom's not home and not answering her cell phone. Sarah even called John David to have him check on her. He told her he didn't think that was a real good idea."

"Smart boy. Your mother has a life, and she hardly ever answers her cell phone." Nash kept his tone mild. "What are you kids going to do when you find her? Ground her?"

Evan stopped at a traffic light and gave him a measuring look. "I'm thirty-one years old, and Mom is the only component of that lifetime that has never changed, never failed, never moved, so to speak. Even though I think the girls carry their concern too far sometimes, I guess the truth is, yeah, if I could ground her, I would. I would make her always be the same, because that's what would be comfortable for me."

Nash wanted to argue, to tell Evan his mother was an adult who deserved to be treated as such, but he couldn't. Because if he were honest with himself, Early staying the same would be comfortable for him, too.

CHAPTER 17

EARLY DIDN'T WANT TO OPEN HER EYES. IF SHE JUST KEPT THEM closed, she was sure she could go back to sleep once she got her shoulder in the right place. The way she was lying, it was as though it was propped on the headboard. She stretched. Or tried to.

Where *was* she, anyway?

No two ways about it, she had to open her eyes.

Oh, no.

"Don't panic. Your virtue's safe." Josh's voice came dryly from somewhere above her. "Sit up. I've got coffee."

She obeyed, finding that the "headboard" was actually the arm of the couch. She took a long sip of the strong brew. "What did I do?"

"Just went to sleep. I tried to wake you, but you weren't having any, so I covered you up and let you sleep." He grinned at her, and even in her muddled state of mind, she wondered why she couldn't fall in love with him, or if not in love, at least into courtship. "I watched an entire chick flick by myself. You're a bad influence."

"It doesn't count unless it made you cry." She yawned. "I'm so sorry."

"Not a problem." He sat beside her. "It was a nice evening."

"It was." She sipped the coffee again, wishing for a toothbrush. She kept extras at her house, but she didn't want to ask Josh if he did. There was something too intimate about that.

The morning sun shot rainbows of light through the leaded glass in the dining area French doors and she blinked. She had to admit, the discussion of hygienic products was probably not more intimate than spending the night on his couch.

Her kids did not call her on a daily basis. They didn't come into her house if no one was there. They had no idea how much money she did or didn't have, nor did she think they were even curious. However, she would be willing to bet at least half of them had called her the night before, and all of them would call today and ask—without *really* asking, of course—where she'd been last night. In their eyes, though her finances and her home were not their business, her personal life definitely was.

She finished her coffee and got up from the couch, pushing her feet into her shoes. "Church this morning." She needed to have a talk with God, which she could do anywhere, but this morning she wanted to have the discussion in the fourth pew on the left. "Thanks for dinner. And breakfast."

"I don't think coffee counts as breakfast." He got her coat out of the entry closet and held it for her.

"It does with me." She kissed him quickly on the cheek. "I'll talk to you later."

It was a long day. Church went later than usual, so by the time Early got home, it was time to open the shop. Customers already waited at the door. Although Francie left at five o'clock, four local quilt club members were still choosing fabric for their next projects a full half hour later.

"Take your time," Early said, "but I'm going to sweep around you."

When she finally walked to the house. Fatigue felt like a too-heavy blanket around her shoulders. She was so hungry she was almost sick with it, but she didn't know where she was going to find the energy to prepare something.

The house was silent when she went in, saved from darkness by the timer-set lights on all the Christmas trees.

She fed the cat and made a sandwich and a cup of hot choco-late. With a bag of potato chips tucked under her arm, she carried the food upstairs, unwilling to spend another night on a couch. Not even her own. And she was almost certain she'd be asleep in minutes.

But she wasn't.

No one had called today, not even the kids she'd been certain would be curious regarding her whereabouts of the night before. The customers who usually spent time in the shop chatting with her and each other had been focused on other things today. Even Francie had been preoccupied, calling Early by Susan's name not once but three times, something she never did.

Early wanted to talk to Nash. She wanted to tell him about meeting Frank Lambert and about being so tired she'd left her coat hanging on a kitchen chair and her clothes on the bathroom floor.

She wanted to know what kind of day he'd had, if he'd eaten well and napped in the afternoon. If he felt more like himself than he had right after the surgery when life was tremulous and scary. "I don't like the dark right now," he said that first night. "Isn't that weird?"

She'd sat beside the bed and held his hand until he slept, and when a nurse offered to close the door against the light, Early had said, "No, leave it open."

Had he played dominoes with his father today and talked to the children?

She sat alone on her bed eating potato chips and watching *Going My Way* and thought how there were areas of her life where she hadn't made any progress at all. It didn't seem to matter how full her days were or how much she liked Josh Walden—the truth was that she was as in love with Nash McGrath as she had ever been.

She knew, because she had lived forty-seven years and counseled four teenage children and watched almost every romantic movie ever released on DVD, that unrequited love was horrendously painful and didn't usually work out well for the one doing the loving. She also knew this knowledge meant nothing; if you loved someone, you just did. If you missed him, nothing filled the place where he belonged. If you wanted to close off the place in your heart where he lived to let the scar tissue heal, you could just forget it; the fissure would pop right back open with hardly any provocation at all.

There would certainly be no harm in checking on him.

He answered his phone on the first ring.

"So, how's the patient?"

His chuckle whispered through the night to warm her. "*Im*patient. How's the quilt shop lady?"

"Okay. Mary Brad and I went to Pleasant Acres yesterday to give away quilts and bags of candy."

He was silent for a couple of beats. "Oh?"

"Yes. The residents liked them. Mrs. Redding lives there."

"Geometry?"

"Uh-huh. And a blind lady with beautiful hands."

"That was a nice thing for you to do. Your quilts are great things."

"Thank you."

He waited again. "And?"

"He was there." She hesitated. "He's awful, Nash." She shook her head. "I don't know how we can tell her."

"We'll find a way. Did you give him a quilt?"

"No, I took it back. The candy, too."

"What did he do?"

"He yelled for me to bring them back, but we just kept walking. I forgot every Sunday school lesson I ever had and every verse of Scripture I ever read about forgiving."

Unrestrained laughter made its way into her senses. "I wish I'd been there. I *should* have been there. He may have been a sperm donor, but I'm her dad."

I'm her dad. Parental love was supposed to be a separate thing from the romantic kind, but it wasn't always. Sometimes the two were inextricably joined, wound together in a way that wouldn't allow disconnection.

"Nash, are you and Ben coming down for Christmas?"

"We are. Even Joe is."

"Do you want to stay for the rest of your convalescence?"

She wasn't sure what she was asking, and his hesitation told her he wasn't positive what he was answering, either.

"I miss Ben," she said. *And you. Always you. And it's not getting any better. Even on days I think it is, I'm fooling myself. Even now, you are the other half of me.*

"Yeah, if it's all right."

His voice sounded lighter. Whether it was with relief or resignation, she wasn't going to argue the point. She felt the same way, whichever it was. "When are you coming?"

"Whenever you want us."

"Tomorrow after your doctor's appointment? You can set up your rehab before you come."

"I'd like that."

On that note, Early was able to sleep.

THE NEXT TWO DAYS GAVE THE ILLUSION—EARLY KNEW IT WAS only an illusion because nothing was ever that easy—of life slipping back into place. Ben was in his room, complaining about his Christmas tree but never turning off the lights. Nash moved into the room Francie had used while she recuperated. For the first time in years, Sarah came home to stay over Christmas break. She helped in the shop during the afternoon and spent evenings with John David. She also went to the administration building and applied to teach at Ridge Community Schools.

"I like it on the Ridge," she said, playing dominoes with her grandparents after dinner. "John David said he'd come to Lexington, but I know he doesn't want to. There's a special education position opening up here. Whether I get it or not could be a different story altogether. Granddad, you have beaten me again!"

"You're not paying attention." Ben grinned at her, putting the black and white tiles back into their wooden box.

"She's got other things on her mind," Francie scolded, smacking Ben on the arm. She got up. "I'm going home. I never meant to stay so late in the first place. That was a delicious supper, Earline."

"It's bribery to keep you working till the Christmas rush is over, which I thought it would be by now. There are only three more days. I don't know what I'd have done without you and Mary Brad and Angie." Early straightened from loading the dishwasher. She was almost certain her back groaned a protest against the motion. "Sure you won't stay for hot chocolate?"

"No, thank you." Francie headed toward the door. "I heard that young man's car in the driveway. You can give him my cup."

"Are you going caroling with us, Gran?" Sarah said, pulling on her coat to walk her grandmother out and her fiancé in. "It's tomorrow night at the nursing home, then we're going across the campus to the assisted living facility and singing there, too. Jessie's coming down to stay over Christmas and she and I will take you out carousing afterward."

"No, thanks. My caroling days are over, I'm afraid. Besides, you girls would make me the designated driver. Where's the fun in that?"

She left on a wave of surprised laughter, one hand hooked in Sarah's elbow. Early stared at the closed door. "Who was that woman and what has she done with my mother?"

"I think more than her ankle has healed over the past months." Ben closed the dominoes box and got up to put them away. "Do you want me to make the hot chocolate, sugar?"

"Sure. Thanks, Ben." Early met Nash's eyes. They were dark and anxious. "She'll see him there. We have to tell her."

"I know."

A few minutes later, Sarah and John David came in together, both of them red-cheeked from the cold. John David took the tray from Ben's hands and carried it to the table. "Is that great big cup mine? I think it has my name on it. Doesn't it, Miss Early?"

Ben walked past him, lifting the cup from the tray. "It has A Soft Place to Fall's name on it. Early puts a couple of fat eighths in them and gives them away as Christmas gifts. I wasn't even a customer and she gave me one. It had a candy bar in it," he added smugly.

"Candy?" Nash looked wounded and somewhat outraged. "She gave you candy? She gives me raw vegetables with yogurt stuff to dip them in."

"Your incision hasn't even healed yet." Early rapped him not-so-lightly on the top of the head. "Sarah and John David, will you sit down? We need to talk to you for a minute. You, too, Ben."

John David drew Sarah's chair out before taking the one beside it. "I've already told you my intentions, and you know I don't have any money."

"They're going to ask me if I'm a virgin." Sarah nodded wisely at him.

"Oh, that's all right then." He smiled beatifically at her. "Are you?"

"None of your business."

Early cleared her throat. "Sarah, other than as a biblical reference, don't use the word *virgin* around your dad and granddad. They have heart conditions."

"Sorry." Sarah exchanged impish looks with Nash and Ben, and Early gave a silent sigh.

Sarah had worshipped her father and grandfather her entire life, and they returned the sentiment. When Nash and Early married, raising Susan's child as well as their own three hadn't been part of the plan, but her integration into the family had been so seamless it was as though she'd been born to them. More than once, Early had caught herself trying to recall her labor with Sarah before remembering she hadn't even been there for her birth. By the time she'd made the middle-of-the-night drive from Lexington with her own three babies, Sarah was lying calm and observant in the hospital nursery. Susan was wide-eyed and frightened in a room down the hall.

Sarah had always been quiet, as different from the others as it was possible to be. Her parents cherished the differences. She was simply their beloved youngest child. Her questions about her biological background had been asked—at least that was how it had seemed—out of idle curiosity, not because her life was lacking.

Early sipped hot chocolate and made herself speak before sheer nerves could make her mouth go dry again. "Do you remember the day you two met?"

Sarah shook her head. "Nope. I think we were in diapers. At least I was. John David had probably graduated to those little bitty underpants with cartoon characters on them."

"I mean the day in the cemetery, when you met again."

"Oh, sure." Sarah's eyes softened when she exchanged another look with John David. "It was a very good day. For us, at least. I don't think Granny Fran enjoyed it a lot. It was the day she broke her ankle, wasn't it?"

"It was, but do you remember asking me about your biological father?"

"Uh-huh. I didn't want to be marrying my brother or something." She addressed her fiancé again, clasping his arm. "You're not, are you? I forgot to ask."

He gave that some thought. "Evan and Logan said I could be theirs as long as I brought my own Lego blocks into the mix, so maybe I am."

"Honey, I think your mother's trying to tell you something." Nash's voice had a quaver in it, and Early gave him a look. This was not, no matter how silly the children acted, a laughing matter.

He returned her look, and she could almost hear the words he didn't say. *Calm down. It'll be all right.*

But would it?

"Sorry, Mama. Go ahead." Sarah's smile was like an embrace. *Child of our hearts, please don't get hurt.* "Your dad and Uncle Joe and I did a little looking around, trying to put the pieces together." Early felt tears pressing behind her eyes. *Oh, Lord, don't let me cry now.*

"What did you find out?" The laughter was gone from Sarah's voice.

Early, who had explained birth, death, and sex to all of her children while scarcely batting an eye, could not speak.

Nash, whose discomfort level and lack of input during those conversations had been grist for the family laughter mill for years, replied quietly. "We found him, baby. You'll see him tomorrow night."

After a few seconds of silence, Sarah looked more curious than concerned. "Does he know about me?"

"Not as far as we know."

Sarah nodded. "Will you show him to me?"

"Yes."

"And will you tell me what you know about him?"

"We'll answer the questions we *can* answer." Nash spoke carefully. "You're old enough to form your own opinions. Unfortunately, your mom and I *aren't* old enough not to try to influence those opinions."

Sarah looked from one to the other of her parents. "Will I like your answers?"

"No." Early and Nash spoke in unison, exchanging wry smiles.

"I wish you had more time to think about it before you see him," Early said.

Sarah shrugged. "I've thought about it off and on since I was in the third grade and Aaron Cruikshank said I must be adopted because my hair was red. Evan told me if you and Daddy were going to adopt somebody, they'd have found somebody smarter who was also a boy. I always figured he was right. I was born in your hearts—goodness knows *where* Aaron Cruikshank and Evan came from." She came around the table to hug her parents. "Thinking about it's not the same as worrying. I didn't worry then and I'm not going to now." She kissed each of them on the cheek and straightened. "I'm going into the living room with John David to watch television and make him wonder about my virtue."

"Let him wonder," Nash warned, his voice thick.

CHAPTER 18

NOT ONLY JESSIE SHOWED UP TO GO CAROLING THE NEXT NIGHT. So did Evan and Logan. Anna and the kids, Logan said, were shopping for Daddy and he wasn't invited.

"She took all four of them?" Early was awestruck. "I don't know what you got her for Christmas, but I'm sure it wasn't enough."

"Spa days. Four of them. Plus a basket of gift cards from every store I could think of that she liked where she wouldn't go and buy stuff for the kids and me."

"Good boy."

Sarah and Jessie looked at their brothers. "You're not going to sing, are you?" said Sarah. "We've *heard* you sing. It's not pretty."

Jessie nodded somberly. "We could be sued, or at the very least you could be jailed for noise pollution. I'm not sure Mama and Daddy would bail you out."

Evan looked past his sisters at John David. "There are, you realize, no givebacks. You get Sarah for keeps and we're throwing Jessie in just for good measure. They're a matched set."

They piled into three cars for the drive to the nursing facility campus. Predictably, with Jessie directing people to cars, Early and Nash ended up together.

"Are you nervous?" Early pulled onto the road and looked over at Nash.

He shrugged. "I am and I'm not. We're all afraid she'll be hurt, which explains the boys driving down to the Ridge in the middle of the week. But even if Lambert ponies up and wants to be the long-lost father in this story, she's still our girl."

"I know." But knowing didn't make her stomach feel any better. It didn't make her heart beat in a normal rhythm or warm her hands even though she was wearing gloves.

"Hey." When they reached the stop sign at the highway, Nash reached over to give her arm a shake. "It'll be fine."

She hoped he was right, but she was reserving judgment on that. Nevertheless, it felt better walking into Last Call with him beside her. She stopped inside the door, grasping his hand. "Let us do what is right, dear Lord," she prayed aloud, "and protect our Sarah from all that could cause her pain."

"Not our will but Yours be done. Amen." Nash's words could have sounded automatic, but they didn't. He was finding his way back.

Early smiled. *Thank You, God.*

Enough people had come to sing that they were able to divide into two choirs. John David kept the McGraths in the same group. "You'll be less musical that way, but the rest of the congregation won't be as likely to get arrested."

The residents were scattered through the facility, but many of them were playing games or watching television in the big common room at its center.

"Mama, your quilts are everywhere. I had to stop Logan from taking one from this innocent old lady. It looked just like the one you made for Abby." Evan spoke under cover of the others' voices. "Where is he?"

"There. At the corner table."

As the group of singers moved around the room, Sarah's siblings situated themselves in a row behind her and John David.

"Circling the wagons," Nash murmured.

Early nodded, recalling with an inward wince the times she'd punished all of them because none of the four would incriminate the others.

Frank Lambert fixed his gaze on Sarah and kept it there, though the scowl that seemed to be habitual remained in place on his fleshy face. His eyes changed, but Early couldn't identify what the alteration of expression meant. He ignored the rest of the singers, including her and Nash, and when they passed, he turned his chair from the table and wheeled away down the corridor.

Sarah watched him go, but her smile remained in place, her hand held tightly in John David's. Outside, before they dispersed to the cars, she hugged her parents. "Thanks for finding out for me."

She sounded fine. More than fine, she sounded relieved. How could she be relieved? Early's faith was strong, she expected prayers to be answered; however, this must be some kind of "yes" record.

Thank You, Lord. Again.

"Now I know, and that's *all* I need to know. You"—she jerked a thumb over her shoulder toward her brothers and Jessie—"and they are my family, and I don't need another one to fill any gaps in my life because there aren't any. Except for that little bitty one between my bottom teeth that could be fixed if I weren't scared of dentists." She hugged Nash again, for a long time. "I love you, Daddy."

"What a suck-up." Evan's voice was rough. "Logan and I have to get back. We'll see you Christmas Eve." He dropped a kiss on the top of Sarah's head. "You'll be all right?"

She nodded, smiling sweetly at him, then turned back to her

parents. "Jessie and I are going out with Noah and John David, Mama. Don't wait up."

Early wouldn't. She hardly ever worried overmuch about her children's social lives. Not that they knew that, of course, and she probably wouldn't tell them; they might decide to give her something to worry about.

"What do you say we go back to your house and wrap presents?" Nash opened the driver's door of her car for her. "Surely with the four hundred things you got for the grandkids, they're not all wrapped."

She started the car and waited till he got in the other side to respond. "You're exaggerating again."

"Maybe. But when I opened the closet door in the room I'm sleeping in, there was no room to put any clothes in it."

"Why should this year be any different? Did you get stuff for them or are you hoping I'm going to share the credit and the bills for what I got?"

"Works for me, and I'll do the same with what I got."

She put the gearshift lever back into Park. "You went shopping?"

"Sort of."

"And?"

"Everybody's covered."

"You're not going to tell me, are you?"

"Nope."

"But you're still going to help me wrap the mess in the closet?"

"I am."

She put the lever back into drive and backed out of the angled parking place. "What a good ex-husband you are."

He laughed, though she didn't think he sounded amused.

"What about Sarah?" She left the parking lot and headed toward home. "Do you think she's as all right as she seemed?"

"Yes."

"Me, too." His gaze met hers. "God is good."

She put her hand over his where it rested on his leg, and he turned his fingers to grasp hers. "All the time."

At home, they drank hot chocolate and wrapped the closet presents, sharing memories of Christmases past. There'd been the year of the bicycles, when Nash had been called to the hospital and Early spent Christmas Eve night assembling two-wheelers and having un-Christian thoughts. Eight years ago when Logan and Anna married and her parents had still been so angry over their daughter's pregnancy they wouldn't talk to the young couple until Evan called them and told them his sister-in-law was crying and it was time for them to grow up. The year of Rosie's death, when they'd all still been fumbling through grief, but Ben had given Early some of the salt and pepper shaker collection and she'd found joy in the pain.

Joy in the pain.

Not for anything would Early live this year over again. There had been too much illness, too many changes, too much hurt. But there had been joy, too, not the least of which was Sarah's reaction to seeing her birth father.

"These are for Angie's kids," she said about the last supply of wrapped gifts as she put them into a wicker clothes hamper.

"What did you get for Angie? She's been a tremendous help in the shop, from what you and Fran said."

"Just money and this hamper. Mother gave her some, too, and so did Mary Brad. When Angie's husband found out she was coming to the shop, I was able to put her on the payroll, but I'm afraid he takes that money as soon as she gets it. We hope she'll keep this to herself, maybe use it to get away someday if that's the path God shows her." She held up the Christmas card containing the cash. "I'll drop the gifts off at her house, but we'll give her this tomorrow. We're closing the shop at noon and coming to the house for lunch." She grinned at him. "It'll be all of us women. You and Ben might want to find somewhere to go."

"We might at that." Nash took money from his wallet and handed it to her. "I know it's something you can't buy insurance for, but I'd give a lot more than this to keep abuse from happening to our girls."

Early tucked the cash into the envelope. "Thank you." She looked into his face. "You look tired. Are you all right?"

"I am and I am." He got to his feet. "I'm going to bed. You?"

"No." She laughed. "I never sleep that much during the holidays. You remember that. It's even worse when you work in retail during the holidays—even if you *want* to sleep, you can't. I think I'll go down to the shop. I haven't finished quilting that wall hanging for Patty Waylon."

He frowned. "I'll go down with you. It's almost midnight."

She waved a dismissive hand. "It's three hundred feet away. I go down almost every night for one thing or another. The path is well-lit and Clarissa is a good watch cat."

His eyebrow lifted. "Clarissa's asleep in the living room."

Early went to him, putting her arms around him. "I'm glad you're here, Nash."

He hugged her hard, and they stood for a moment, rocking back and forth in the way of people who fit together regardless of the ravages of time and circumstances.

"Get some sleep. Tomorrow will be a busy day." She kissed his cheek.

Nash turned his head enough that their lips caught and held for a warm, teasing moment. She felt heat come into her cheeks and looked down, feeling like a hormonal teenager.

He cleared his throat. "Well, do me a favor and carry your cell phone in your pocket when you walk down there. I know the ice has supposedly all melted from the other day, but it only takes a little piece to make you fall down. Whether we like it or not, we're approaching the age of bones breaking a little easier than they used to." He held up his hands in a gesture of helplessness. "I know, I know. It ticks me off, too, but what are you gonna do?"

She laughed. "You are such a goofball. I would carry my phone, but the battery's dead."

He rolled his eyes. "Why am I not surprised?" He reached behind her to where his cell lay on the counter. "Here, take mine."

"What if one of your women calls?"

"It's either a wrong number or one of our daughters checking on us. It's on vibrate anyway. You won't even know if it rings."

The night was clear. The older grandkids would be disappointed if it wasn't a white Christmas. They'd watched enough of their grandparents' old movies to think snow, the birthday of Jesus, and Santa Claus all went together. Early pulled her coat closer about herself as she jogged down the path toward the shop. In December, clear often meant cold. Tonight was no exception to that particular rule.

She disabled the alarm and stepped inside, turning on the row of lights that illuminated the center of the store. She moved through the room, spending fifteen minutes doing the straightening and set-up she usually did before opening in the morning. She stood still at the display of batiks and drew a deep breath. The scent, sight, and sensation of a fabric store, particularly her own, were some of her favorite things.

Near the back of the silent building, past Francie's Rack of Rulers but before Rosie's Corner, she stopped, her hand going into her pocket to grasp Nash's phone. The back of her neck prickled.

Something wasn't right.

A lot of vandalism had occurred along the Ridge lately. Mary Brad lost a few pedigreed chickens and the door off their coop only a few weeks ago, although Reginald had escaped unscathed. But crime, the stuff of which television shows and dark, fearsome headlines were made, didn't happen here. Or, if it did, it happened over in the mean little streets of Over Yonder or in the trailer park just outside of Pleasant Hill where the tenants rented by the week and never stayed long. Not here on the winding bucolic road between Stringtown Proper and Four Corners.

All the same, Early felt something different inside the shop. Something colder than the thermostat setting registered. She wasn't sure, as she stood still, barely breathing, if she felt some*thing* or some*one*. She hadn't locked the door after herself when she came in, but surely she would have heard someone follow her. Wouldn't she?

"Angie?" she said aloud, then shook her head at her own silliness. Angie had left with Francie hours ago.

Unable to shake the heebie-jeebies, Early turned back toward the front door. It would be just as easy to finish Patty's wall hanging before the shop opened in the morning.

The man stepped out from behind Jessica's Shelf, knocking a few of the brightly colored bolts of fabric to the floor as he straightened and approached Early. He shuffled when he walked, and he wore a long coat with a hood, but there was no disguising who the visitor was. Early reached for the receiver in her pocket, but she didn't even know how to operate it, much less what to dial so that the phone in the house would ring.

"What do you want?" she said, surprised her voice worked.

Frank Lambert snorted. "I wanted to be left alone, but you couldn't do that, could you? You had to come snooping around the other day, asking questions you didn't need the answers to. Then you had to bring that girl in, the one that looks like her mother. The retard."

The rage leapt, seething, into her throat, but so did something else. Fear? Early didn't think she could talk; her heart was beating too hard, her breath coming so quick and shallow she thought she might hyperventilate.

"I still don't know why you're here." When it finally came, her voice was high and thin.

"To finish things."

"Finish?" What did he mean? "There's nothing to finish."

"Sure there is. I get lonesome, you know, there at the Last Call."

...even then he's alone. No one visits him. Joe's words flitted through the back of her mind.

"I'm sure you do. Everyone gets lonely." *Please come, Nash. Please.* "What does that have to do with me? With coming into the shop in the middle of the night."

"I wasn't going to. I was going to go to the house, but Nash is there. And his old man. I didn't want to meet up with them. The McGrath boys always thought they was heroes. For all I know, they still do." He sounded composed, almost friendly.

Early concentrated on not gagging. "You're not answering my questions."

"The retard was real good company. After she had that kid, though, she didn't want nothing to do with me no more."

Oh, God.

As if in answer to the prayer or protest, whichever it was, calm descended. Her breathing and heartbeat slowed. Even the nausea that had clawed the back of her throat dissipated. Her voice was her own again, steady and cold.

"Did you hurt her?"

"Huh?"

"Did you hurt my sister? You know, the one who never hurt anyone in her life, who had more love and decency in her little finger than you've ever had in your entire soul. The *retard*." Early didn't think she'd ever said the word out loud before. Even in this eerily calm place she found herself, she hoped she never said it again.

The phone in her coat pocket vibrated against her hip. Nash was wrong. She did know when it rang.

"She wouldn't let me." Lambert shook his head.

"Let you what?"

"You know what I'm talking about. She said good mommies didn't do that, but I told her she was too dumb to be a good mommy anyway so she could. She always liked it in the water, so I got her to go into the creek, told her we could just go for a swim. But then she kept fighting and fighting."

That was when Early knew. She drew in a deep, gasping breath. "You killed her."

"Nah. Well, maybe. I held her under a while so she'd stop fighting and then she wouldn't wake up. But it was her fault." He spoke casually, lifting his beefy hands in a "what could I do?" gesture.

A gun, small enough that it didn't even look overly scary, was palmed in one of those hands, but it barely registered with Early. *Oh, Susie.* The pain almost doubled her over, and she reached to grasp the end of the shelf nearest her. Early had convinced herself over the years that Susan hadn't suffered before she died in the water, her favorite place. But she had. She had. *Oh, Susie. Dear Lord, did You hold her in Your arms and take her home?*

"You need…" She stopped, swallowed, tried again. "You need to leave here and never come back. There's no more damage you can do here."

Except to Sarah. Please, God, not Sarah.

"But I'm not done, Mrs. McGrath." He moved closer. "If I can't have one sister, I'll settle for the other'n."

She backed away, releasing the shelf. And saw the gun again. It didn't look small anymore. "Get out," she said, "before it's too late." Hysteria bubbled in her throat—Early was afraid of guns at the best of times; this wasn't one of those. *He can't shoot me in here. Blood will get all over the fabric and someone will have to clean it up. And it's Christmas. I can't die at Christmas. The grandkids would never get over it. They're little. They want white Christmases and birthday cakes for Jesus, not blood-spattered memories.*

"I will die," she said aloud, though the voice seemed to be coming from somewhere else, "before you touch me."

And she walked past him. If anyone could have interrupted the scene and asked her, she'd have said she was too completely terrified to move; that only happened in movies made for television. But she did it. Even though her feet felt as though they were full of lead, she walked toward the front door. One step at a time. Right. Left. Right. Left. *I will fear no evil, for Thou art with me...*

She sensed rather than saw the movement from outside, and her dread increased as she approached the door. *Don't come in. Please don't let him come in. I'll come out. It will be all right.*

The door opened despite her prayer. She saw Nash's face as he stepped inside the door. He smiled when he saw her, relief slipping across his features. "Why didn't you answer the phone?" he said, closing the door behind him.

From behind her came a metal-against-metal click. A small sound that became huge, dark, and ugly.

She leaped. Even with leaden feet, she was able to leap. She crashed into Nash, throwing them both against the heavy door.

She screamed, *"Noooooooo,"* from a throat that felt like splintered glass.

An explosive noise, nothing like the popping sound of hunting rifles in the woods, filled the air around her and something slammed into her back. She wasn't sure, in that endless instant before everything went black, if it hurt or not.

CHAPTER 19

"HE'S HER HUSBAND AND HE HAS PRIVILEGES IN THIS HOSPITAL. IF you want to argue with him, go right ahead, but you're going to have to wait a while. I've got things to do in there and I can use his help." Ross Michaels glared at the emergency room clerk and the sheriff's deputy in turn, then nodded toward the nearest cubicle. "This way, Dr. McGrath."

Nash didn't correct the "he's her husband" part of Dr. Michaels' statement. "John David," he said, looking over his shoulder, "will you and Noah call the boys and Fran?" *And take care of the girls.* He knew he didn't have to say that. *And pray.* But he didn't have to say that, either. "My daughters can give you the information you need," he told the clerk kindly, though he didn't feel kind.

Nothing like kind. He felt agonizingly angry. And scared. *Oh, holy and merciful God, I'm scared.*

"Dr. McGrath, I need to know if you're going to be all right in here." Dr. Michaels' voice was crisp, but his eyes were warm. "Mrs. McGrath is our first concern."

"And mine."

He'd ridden in the ambulance with Early, holding her hand

and keeping his mouth shut because the EMT had more expertise in trauma medicine than he did. Years back, Janine Cramer had taught him all about getting in the way of someone doing their job when she hauled him into the hospital corridor and told him to butt out and shut up. He'd given her a filthy look that promised later retribution, but was smart enough not to deliver on the look.

"Vitals?" he asked once, tersely. The EMT answered just as succinctly, never taking his eyes from what he was doing.

"You knew what to do. That helps, sir."

Nash knew that. He'd been able put pressure on the horrible wound on her back and to count her respirations and her pulse. He could check the response of her eyes and beg her to wake up. *Don't leave us, Early. We can't be without you.* He knew her blood type and her medical history up to and including the chicken pox scar on her forehead. When the EMT asked about medications, he told him which daily vitamins were in the divided box in the drawer in the kitchen, about the water pill she swallowed every morning because it helped keep her blood pressure within the safe range. He could even, disjointedly, pray, although he didn't find words for what he asked for. *Oh God oh God oh God.*

Dr. Michaels was beside Early now, listening, sensing, looking with a narrowed gaze at the evidence before him. "Has she regained consciousness at all?"

"No, sir, but the numbers are good. BP's 100/60 and steady…"

The numbers are good. Nash stopped listening to what the professionals beside the narrow ER bed said to each other and stepped back to take deep breaths and stay out of the way. A hyperventilating family member was the last thing any of them needed, particularly Early.

"How is she on allergies again?" asked Dr. Michaels, looking over at him, his eyes above the mask alert and assessing.

"None." Nash stepped forward again. *The numbers are good.* He held onto the thought. "Well, dusting."

"What?" The young physician's eyebrows drew together in confusion, but the women on the trauma team all chuckled as one.

"She always says she's allergic to dusting." *If you'll just be all right, I'll dust for you for the rest of our lives. I'll drive down from Lexington every Wednesday. You can cook and I'll clean and we'll go to Wednesday night services at the church at the Corners. We'll laugh about this someday. Hear me, Early, please. Laugh with me.*

He listened, but not really, to what they said as they worked over Early.

The numbers are good.

"...through and through..."

Nash interrupted. "What?"

"There's an exit wound," a nurse explained.

He already knew what "through and through" meant. Now he wanted to know what the bullet from the little gun had damaged in its path.

This was why doctors didn't take care of their loved ones. It was why his professor had said he shouldn't practice family medicine. Nash had never been able to separate the ailment from the patient. He hadn't sutured his children when they'd needed stitches or observed at their appendectomies. He'd stood across their beds from Early and they'd met each other's eyes and shared their strength, making them into a most formidable parental team.

Later—he didn't know how much later because time had somehow become irrelevant—he heard Early's voice, and wondered for a tortured instant if he only thought he had because he wanted to so much. But then he heard it again.

"Early?" He stepped between the nurses. "You're at the hospital and you're going to be all right. Are you in pain?"

"Nash? You all right?" She sounded whispery. In a better time and place, the tone would have been sultry. Now it was…hurt, and it wrapped itself as firmly around his heart as sultriness would have.

"I am."

"You taking care of me?"

"Nope. Dr. Michaels is."

She mumbled something and he bent closer so he could hear. He laughed and looked over at the other doctor. "She says you're the cute one. I'm not sure where that leaves me."

"I've heard stories." The young doctor's grin stretched his mask. "I tried getting them to call me Dr. Adorable here, but the best this staff came up with was Dr. Pain-in-the-Neck."

"I've heard that one, too."

"On the nine-lives scale, I'd say you used up a couple of them tonight, Early, but you should have several left." Dr. Michaels returned his attention to the patient. "We're going to finish cleaning up and closing up the wound and then we're going to keep you at least overnight so you can have some serious pain meds—which you're going to need. The bullet did a little muscle damage, but not much, and it missed everything vital. You'll be in for some therapy to get your arm and shoulder moving right, but I'd say the only physical reminder you'll have of this night will be a rather impressive scar. A plastic surgeon can pretty that up some, too, if it matters to you."

"I'll go tell the kids." Nash bent to press his lips to Early's forehead. "I'll see you upstairs."

When he entered the emergency room waiting area, it looked like a family reunion. Even the grandkids were there, wrapped in quilts their grandmother had made for them and sleeping two to a couch. Fran looked as though she'd aged ten years.

"Daddy?" Sarah's voice trembled, and he went to her first, to put his arms around her and hold her close. He knew this child's overdeveloped sense of responsibility. She might very well take it upon herself to think it was her fault her biological father was crazy.

"She'll be fine," he promised, reaching past Sarah to grasp Fran's hand and looking around at the crowd of people. Even Joe was there, standing a little apart with his arm around Mary Brad. "She'll be awfully sore, and she's going to be the care recipient for a while instead of the caregiver."

"That'll tick her off." Evan's voice was thick.

Everyone tried to laugh, though the effort was feeble at best.

"What do you want us to do, Dad?" asked Logan, lifting Fiona into his arms as she struggled to a sitting position on the couch.

"Go home, or back to your mom's if you want to stay closer."

"What are you going to do?" Jessie clung to Noah's hand. Nash thought abstractedly that he'd never seen his oldest daughter dependent on anyone for anything.

But, she'd never almost lost her mother, either.

"I'll be here." He let go of Sarah to hug Jessie.

"Grandpa?"

Nash knelt to Abby's six-year-old level. "What, baby?"

"What about Christmas? There can't be Christmas without Nana."

He couldn't speak. He pulled Abby to him and bent his head until he could gather his composure.

"You know," he said finally, his voice sounding as splintered as he felt, "you're right, Abby." He looked around at the faces of his family, registering the fear, hope, and relief he saw in varying stages. "When Nana comes home, then we'll have Christmas."

They joined hands then, forming a circle of gratitude. John David's voice broke as he gave thanks for the sparing of Early's life. "Jesus loves me," Abby sang in a voice pure with innocence, and they all joined in. It was a night, after all, for caroling.

"YOU CAN LEAVE THE HOSPITAL," SAID DR. MICHAELS, "BECAUSE your ex-husband's a doctor, your son's a doctor, your daughter-in-law's a nurse, and your mother's pretty terrifying on her own. Oh, and your family has declared that it's Christmas Eve. You are not to do *anything* that will risk opening that wound, including crawling around under Christmas trees with the numerous and sundry grandchildren I've seen darting around here. The boy—Jacob?—told me he had it on good authority that Santa Claus wouldn't come if you weren't home. I don't want to be responsible for that."

"Thank you. I promise I'll get better right away. Are you working tomorrow? We'll be celebrating Christmas." If she was very calm and looked him in the eye, she told herself, he wouldn't be able to tell she was in pain.

"Yes."

Early smiled. Evan usually worked for the same reason—he wasn't a husband or a father. "Would you join us for dinner?" she asked. "We're loud, but the food's good, and no one will get mad if you have to bolt from the table in the middle of Ben saying grace. He's used to it. I think he interrupts himself if no one else does."

"I'd like that."

"Evan was awful, wasn't he?" She wasn't sure why she knew that, although at one point in her tour through the emergency room, she'd had a vague sense of loud voices. But she'd been the mother of sons for over thirty years—yelling often meant nothing. Had she been able to rise above the pain and the medication, she'd have told the shouters to take it outside.

"No. He was someone concerned for his mother." The doctor frowned at her. "You're still hurting a lot, Early. Why don't you stay here with us at least one more day? You can have Christmas in the visitors' lounge. Your family and the staff can all be there."

"I have a daughter who will feel responsible because her biological father is the one who shot me," she said. "I need to show her this is nothing, just a big, bloody mosquito bite. She has to know I'm all right, and that's not going to happen while I'm in here."

Dr. Michaels sighed. "Nash said the same thing. She's a lucky girl."

"We're the lucky ones."

By the time Early was home and in the hospital bed that seemed to have taken up permanent residence in the old dining room, she wasn't all that certain about the lucky part. Pain throbbed through her back. "It feels like a toothache," she murmured as Evan laid a pillow behind her and gave her two pills along with a glass of water.

"Try to sleep, Mom." The distress in his voice made her want to comfort him. Mothers weren't supposed to worry their children. This was all backwards.

Sometime later—she couldn't have said how much time—she woke to find Anna leaning over her, her light brown hair in a loose ponytail. She wore scrubs with reindeer on them. Her cool fingers were on Early's wrist, her brown eyes assessing. "How you doing, Mama?"

"Better." She turned her hand to give Anna's a squeeze. "You look tired."

"I just came off a twelve-hour shift with a little overtime thrown in on each end. It was the only way to spend our family Christmas with the kids."

Early smiled. "These are such good times. I'm so grateful you're willing to share them with us. And grateful to your parents for spending this winter in Sedona so we get all the holidays without feeling selfish, but don't tell them I said so."

"I won't, but my mother said for you and Nash to do double on the spoiling." Anna looked thoughtful. "She didn't say a word about babysitting, though. Are you and she in cahoots in the 'I've raised my children, you raise yours' club?" Her voice lowered to a whisper. "Santa Claus is in the living room as we speak. I wish you could see Logan and Evan putting together Lucas's tricycle. They don't look like men with a whole host of college degrees between them."

Early laughed, finding relief in being able to do so without stabbing pain—those must be powerful meds she was taking. "Nash always looked the same way, so they came by it honestly. Is he supervising?"

"Just watching. He's worried about you." Anna kissed her cheek. "I'm going to send him in here. That way, I can lie on the couch in the living room and pretend I'm not falling asleep. Nash can have the recliner in here with you."

"'Night, Anna. I'm glad you're here." Early could barely keep her eyes open.

A moment later, Nash's kiss was quick and warm on her forehead. "Sleep," he whispered.

She heard the creak of the recliner as he settled into it, then the warm firmness of his hand around hers. She would be able to rest now.

Or almost now. She opened her eyes. "Sarah?"

"She's okay. She's with John David and his family tonight, but will be here in the morning."

"What about Frank?" She wasn't afraid, but she wanted to know where he was.

"In jail."

"What will happen to him?"

"I don't know, and I don't particularly care."

"Has Sarah said anything?"

"Not about him."

"Don't let her take the blame."

"I won't. None of us will." He lifted her hand and kissed her palm. "Now, get some sleep. The grands won't care if you're awake or not when they rip into that stuff under the tree. They were only concerned with you being here, not whether you actually got in on any of the fun."

"I've never slept on Christmas Eve, even pretend ones." She tried to chuckle, but couldn't seem to get enough breath.

"Me, either." He kept her hand in his. "But we're not too old to learn."

CHAPTER 20

"YOU MUSTN'T WAKE NANA." THE ADMONISHING VOICE FILTERED into the room and Nash listened in drowsy contentment. "She and Grandpa were up late helping Santa Claus. We'll eat breakfast first this year. That way, Mommy and Uncle Evan can sleep and Uncle Evan won't be a bear."

"I'm never a bear. Aunt Jessie's just a pain." Evan's growl came from farther away. "But she's right about Nana and Grandpa, kids. They're tired. Where's Fiona?"

"She was right here a second ago."

Nash opened his eyes in time to catch his youngest grandchild as she climbed into his lap. "Hey, there, sugar. Did you get away?"

Fiona kissed him wetly, then stretched chubby arms toward Early.

"Stay with me," he urged, nuzzling her neck. "Nana's sleeping."

"No, she's not." The bed buzzed as Early raised it to an upright position. She patted the bed beside her in invitation. "Want to sit with me, baby Fee?"

"No, she doesn't." Logan came into the room, Lucas on one

hip, and reached for his daughter with his free arm. "You should still be sleeping, both of you."

Nash scowled at his younger son. "Is your grandfather up?"

"Yes, but—"

"Is Granny Fran here? I could have sworn I heard her voice a little bit ago."

"Well, yeah, but—"

"Last time I looked, they were even older than your mother and I, believe it or not. Are the kids champing at the bit?"

Logan rolled his eyes. "Oh, yeah. We're thinking of having Jacob arrested just to restrain him."

Nash met Early's eyes, exchanging unspoken promises. "Then give us a few minutes and we'll be there."

"Should Mom move that far?"

"She should." Early swung her legs over the side of the bed, catching her breath for a moment. "Clear the couch for Dad and me."

They'd sat on the couch together for thirty-one Christmas mornings, hoping the phone would hold off ringing on his on-call years and drinking their coffee as the children opened presents. This year wasn't going to be any different. Nash felt relief move through him in a glad rush.

"You okay?" he asked, when they'd both managed to brush their teeth and were moving toward the living room. "Weren't we in our forties just last week? What happened?"

"I'm not sure, but this week's bound to be better."

When they were seated and Jessie and Sarah were handing out gifts, Nash reached for Early's hand. "You know, don't you?" He spoke under cover of the noise and the music that filled the room.

"Probably. I'm the mom. I know everything. But exactly what are you referring to?"

He grinned at her. How could he have ever thought there

could be a happy moment without her? "That I love you," he said. "That I always have even when I didn't know it myself."

"Oh." Her expression didn't change, but her eyes did; they seemed to light from within. She brought her free hand to his face, shaping his cheek and scraping his morning beard lightly with her fingers. "Yes, I know that. I love you, too."

SARAH PASSED AROUND FRAMED COPIES OF A DRAWING DONE IN vibrant colors. It was of an eclectic sort of family tree, with acorns with children's names and apples for men and pretty flowers for women. There was an especially lovely white rose for Susan. "You will note," Sarah said, "that there is no leaf or flower for Frank Lambert on the tree. Not even a bruised-up windfall. As far as I'm concerned, he needs never be mentioned again unless he's brought to justice for what he did to both my mothers. I know you've worried about me—that's what families do—but I'm going to be fine. I love all of you, even Evan." She smiled at the oldest of her brothers. "You will hang this, right?"

"Yup." He stood long enough to give her a hug. "There's a spot right in the back of my closet that's just crying out for it."

Early met Nash's gaze, certain her smile was as wide as his. Whatever else came to pass with Frank Lambert, their little girl was going to be all right.

Nash bought them all a Florida beach vacation. "I rented the house for the last two weeks of June and the first two of July," he said, "so everyone will have time to arrange to be there part of the time. The house is huge and there's even a guesthouse on the property in case we have to send Evan and Logan outside—"

"As usual," chorused everyone except the young men in question.

"I don't know what they're talking about, do you?" asked

Logan, refilling his brother's coffee cup. "Did you see that game Jacob got? We'll be able to play with it as soon as he loses interest."

"That's good. If it wasn't for your kids, we'd never get anything fun." Evan pulled Fiona into his lap. "Even this one's growing on me."

"Be careful," Anna warned. "She bites and she hasn't had all her shots."

Early laughed. Even though things were a little foggy, a euphoric feeling induced no doubt by whatever medications she'd been given, the McGrath Christmas morning was as boisterous and loving as it always was.

Nash spoke close to her ear. "Will you come to the beach?"

She turned her head to meet his gaze. She knew his gift was to her more than the others, because she was the one who thrived on a house full of people and noise. Its emptiness had been what she hated about the house in Canterbury Crossing, although she hadn't realized it at the time. She loved visiting Logan and Anna there, now that it was full of children and laughter and the occasional water fight and temper tantrum.

"Open yours," she said, pointing at the flat package on the table beside him.

He squinted at it. "I have no clue what this is. You haven't given me a comic book for Christmas since the kids were little and we didn't have any money. You know, back when I gave you —" He stopped. "What *did* I give you?"

She grinned at him. "Logan."

"You should have taken the coal in your stocking instead, Mama," said Jessie, helping Abby dress her new Barbie in beach clothing. "It would have been less trouble and you could have used it in the fireplace." She held the doll up for her niece's approval. "Keep this away from Jacob or he'll pull off her arms and legs and burn her hair up."

"I can't play with matches," said Jacob seriously, "but how do you take her arms and legs off?"

"You don't," his father advised, "or Aunt Jessie will be taking you to court."

"We didn't have a fireplace till we moved to Canterbury Crossing, so the coal wouldn't have done any good anyway," Early said.

"Remember that space heater we had in our first apartment?" Nash shook his head. "We had to put chicken wire around it to keep the boys from crawling into it. Then you decorated the chicken wire at Christmas because we didn't have either the room or the money for a tree."

Early laughed. "Medication softens memories. It probably wasn't that much fun."

"Sure, it was." He held her gaze, his gift from her half-opened in his hands. "Wasn't it?"

"Yes." And for a moment she sat quiet, reveling in what was in his eyes. Then she pointed at the present in his hands. "Open it."

He tore off the remainder of the wrapping and looked down at the brochures he held. "Alaska?"

"Or anyplace else you'd like to go. I don't know anything about cruises, so I just picked up the materials at the travel agency. We can't go this year, since we seem to be grounded by gunshots and surgery, but maybe next." She heard the tremor in her voice and realized she was nervous. What if she'd read more into the closing gap between them than there actually was?

"Just us?"

"Yes."

"Over the holidays?"

"Yes. We can leave on Christmas afternoon if you want to, as soon as dinner's over and the dishes are done."

"You going to wear a bikini?"

"Not on your life. I have twenty extra pounds and stretch marks from here to—" She stopped, suddenly aware their conversation had an interested audience. "Never mind. You know where I have pounds and stretch marks."

He knew where all her scars and imperfections were, just as she could locate his with her eyes closed. But, like his need for quiet and hers for noise, the flaws were part of the beloved whole, no more important than they allowed them to be.

"Maybe we should fix breakfast," Francie suggested, getting to her feet. "Come on, children." She shook a finger at Evan and Logan. "You boys stop throwing that ball in the house. Take it outside."

It was amazing how quickly a room could empty.

Early met Nash's eyes, looking for—what? They'd already professed their love; that wasn't in doubt. So what was she trying to find? "Well?" Her voice still sounded wobbly to her own ears.

The brochures slid to the floor when he took her hands in his. "I left you," he said quietly, "and at some point over years past, I left God, too. I've finally learned that I need you both. God already said yes. How about you? Will you marry me?"

For a moment, Early gave thought to the hard journey toward being alone and of the satisfaction it had brought. She could scarcely bear the idea of leaving this house, her shop, the Ridge itself, but Nash's practice was still in Lexington and she would never ask him to leave it.

He was offering her their old life, the one she hadn't wanted to give up.

The one she didn't want back.

Guide me, Lord. Help me to say the right things.

But Nash wasn't finished. "Evan would love to have my office."

She couldn't have heard right. Nash loved his practice. For that matter, he loved the corner office with warm cherry furniture and a view of the park. She shook her head, wondering if the medication had affected her hearing. "What?"

"I thought I could spend the next six months or so leaving the practice and finding one here on the Ridge that might have room for a set-in-his-ways family physician."

"You'd leave Lexington?"

"In a heartbeat, and mine's pretty good these days, by the way."

His answer made her own heart stumble and skip. Her cheeks trembled when she smiled at him. "If it takes a while, I could spend time with you there, too. Mother and Angie could run the shop."

"We could have fun up there, knowing we always had this to come back to."

She sobered. "I'm not the same person you left, Nash."

He turned, taking care not to jostle her, and framed her face with his hands. "Yes, you are. And you are more than you were then, too. How exciting is that?" He smiled, stroking her hair back from her face.

She needed a trim, and her roots were probably showing, too; it seemed as though they usually were. But that was one of those imperfections she'd just thought about. One of those things that didn't really matter.

"I'm not the same man who left you, either. At least, not exactly." He took one of her hands and held it on his chest. "I have practically a new heart, and it's all yours."

"Let's take it slower this time." She smiled into his eyes. "Nobody's pregnant, nobody's parents are mad, nobody has a scholarship to the University of Kentucky he's trying to keep. So let's take our time, the way we didn't get the chance to when we were young."

"I'm good with that." He smiled back. "As soon as you're ambulatory, what do you say we have a date?"

"All right."

He kissed her then. More than once. Until the family started drifting back in and their sons set about telling them they were going about it all wrong.

It was a wonderful Christmas, even though Early ended the day exhausted and in considerable pain.

"The reason we celebrate Christmas," she murmured to Nash, "is the new beginning mankind received. The baby who grew up to teach about so many things, not the least of which was forgiveness. I feel as though we've gotten a new beginning today, too."

His gaze met and tangled with hers. The expression in his eyes was warm and mesmerizing, like a slow dance on a summer's eve. "We have."

It was a promise.

CHAPTER 21

SPRINGTIME

FREEDOM.

"Divorce isn't anything I ever wanted." Angie pressed triangles of different shades of blue to the planning wall. "It's getting better, but I'm still scared."

Early smiled at her from where she was sewing beads on what seemed like a hundred yards of candlelight satin. "Been there, done that. You'll be fine."

"But you got married again, to the same person," said Angie. "Do I need some yellow with this?"

"Only if yellow feels right." Early wouldn't add yellow—traditional blue and white was her favorite combination—but it wasn't her quilt. "And he's not quite the same person. Neither am I."

"Do you think he and I could change enough to ever try again?" Angie put some yellow on the wall and immediately took it off.

No! But Early couldn't say that out loud. "I don't know," she said cautiously instead, "but you have to be careful what your kids see, Ange. It made it easier for us, that the kids and grand-kids never saw us as separate—we just lived in different places for a while."

They still did sometimes. Three months after a marriage cere-mony one cold March Sunday when all the children had been able to attend, Nash worked occasionally in Lexington in addition to three days a week in the practice he and Ross had opened on the Ridge.

"They don't miss him. They've even stopped jumping if they hear voices raised." Angie sighed. "I don't miss him, either, to tell the truth. I just don't much like being alone." She put another yellow piece on the wall and took it down. "Yuck. I guess these blues just weren't meant to have yellow with them." She stood still for a moment, a rarity in itself. "The kids and I, we're blues. We don't need a yellow to make us complete."

"Good girl." Francie spoke from where she stood at the counter folding fat quarters. Her gaze met Early's. "And I'm sorry, Earline, that when you and Susan were children, I didn't realize not everyone needs a yellow. We'd have been all right, but I just didn't have the courage to leave him after Susan was born the way she was. So I blamed her for how hard our lives were." She stroked a hand over a red print to smooth it. Again and again and again. "I can't tell her I'm sorry."

"She didn't know, Mama." Early thought she might be stretching the truth a bit here, but it seemed necessary. "Susie always knew she was loved." There, that part *was* true.

"I hope you're right. Maybe I can make things right with Sarah, anyway."

"You already have." Early grinned at her. "Of course, if you wanted to sew some of these beads on this dress, that would make things even righter. The wedding's twenty-two hours away and I swear I still have a thousand or so left to sew on."

Francie laughed. "All right."

"I do have a question, though." Early put down the satin. "Who's the man in the picture in your wallet?"

Her mother looked startled. "You didn't recognize him?"

"No. He seemed familiar, but I didn't know who it was."

Francie's smile still glimmered, though the expression in her eyes was far away. "It's Henry Fonda, the actor, when he was young."

"Oh, well, that clears it all up."

"When you girls were little, *Grapes of Wrath* was on television, and Susan kept running up to the screen and patting Henry Fonda's face and calling him Daddy. Since her own father didn't have any time for her, I figured Mr. Fonda wouldn't mind if Susie pretended and I went along with her."

Early remembered how mesmerized Susan had been by old movies. Since she'd liked them, too, she'd never given it any thought, nor had she ever noticed a marked preference on her sister's part for Henry Fonda. "I thought I knew her so well, but I never picked up on that."

"Oh, my." Mary Brad's voice came from where she was arranging spring-colored quilts in the front window. "What a party we have descending on us. Did they bring a bus?"

Early set the dress aside and went to look, smiling at the sight of her entire family approaching the store. Ben walked between her sons. The grandchildren, complete with the new puppy they insisted really was housebroken, ran around the laughing cluster of adults.

"Everyone's here for the wedding. Hide the dress, Mama. John David's with them and Sarah's being very traditional about what he can and can't see."

Nash brought up the rear of the group, walking with his arm around Sarah and his head tilted toward hers. When they were nearly there, he lifted his head and his eyes met Early's through the small-paned front window of A Soft Place to Fall. He kissed Sarah's forehead and jogged ahead of the crowd so he was first in the door. He snagged Early's waist with one arm, drawing her full-length against him to kiss her as family members crowded into the store after him. "Hey, Mrs. Dr. McGrath, did you miss me?"

"Not really," she admitted, smiling at him. "It's been way too busy here for that. But that doesn't make me any less glad to see you."

He looked at the throng milling through the store. "Has this family grown or is it my imagination?"

"It's growing, but mostly they're just getting louder." Early lifted Fiona into her arms, rejoicing in the lack of pain in the movement.

"Are you looking forward to the beach house?" His gaze still held hers.

"I am." Still holding Fiona, she bent to hug the other three grandchildren as they surrounded her. When she straightened, she hooked her free arm around Nash's neck. "As long as I get to begin and end my days with you, Dr. Adorable, my cup is full."

THE WEDDING OF SARAH AND JOHN DAVID WAS BEAUTIFUL, filled with tears and laughter that would become the sweetest of memories. Fiona followed her older sister up the aisle, industriously picking up the flower petals Abby dropped. Jacob and Lucas were so involved playing jacks they had to be told three times to take their ring pillows and enter the procession. Ushers Evan and Logan argued over who "had to" escort their mother to her seat until she smacked them with the little silk purse that held her tissues and walked into the sanctuary between them. Photographs of Susan and John David's parents stood on the altar between lit candles, ribbon-tied white carnations lying in front of the frames.

Nash walked Sarah up the aisle. Joe performed the ceremony, asking "who shares this woman with this man" and responding with the rest of the McGraths and Francie, "Her family does."

Members of Sarah's class at the Lexington school where she'd taught since she'd earned her special education degree, led by their teaching assistants and joined by eager flower girls and ring bearers, sang "Jesus Loves Me."

Early and Nash left the reception before it was over, driving home through soft twilight. They changed clothes and went outside, where Early watered flowers and talked coaxingly to the plants in the garden while Nash sat on the glider and looked up Scripture for the next morning's service. He was the liturgist at church, a job he took as seriously as any he'd ever undertaken.

Standing at the edge of the porch, she watched him as he read. So much had changed in a year. Divorce, illness, injury, and secrets revealed had changed the fabric of their lives, creating ragged gaps in the seams Early had thought irreparable. But mend them they had, and the stitches required had only served to make the whole cloth stronger.

A sudden memory made her laugh aloud.

"What's funny?" He laid his glasses on the table beside him but kept the Bible open in his lap.

"I was thinking," she said, "of the day you came around the side of the house and your dad accidentally sprayed you with the hose."

Nash snorted. "I'm not entirely convinced it was an accident. Too bad a cold shower didn't wake me up earlier, though, isn't it? Like before I left. Before we got a divorce."

She sat beside him, giving the glider a push with one bare foot. "I'm not so sure it *is* too bad."

"How do you figure?"

"Well, we were better off than most divorced people because we were still friends. But the truth is that we needed to change. Being apart made that possible in a way it might not have been if we'd still been accountable to each other at the end of the day."

He smiled, his dark eyes resting on her like a lazy caress she felt right down to her bones. "I'm still a doctor who spends too much time involved with work. You're still the ultimate caregiver. How have we changed?"

"Well, for me there's the quilt shop. This house. The classes I teach both here and at the community college—good heavens, do you remember when I didn't think I'd even get my diploma? I was the only person in the GED class who was a nursing mother."

"One who ironed my shirts and lab coats in your off time."

She ignored his interruption. "One of my favorite things about you is the kind of doctor you are. You're caring and generous with your time and your knowledge. You even do your own call-backs and have been known to make a house call or two. I've always loved you for that, but I didn't love that husband and father always took the back burner to everything medical in your life. He doesn't anymore and we all appreciate that."

He took her hand. "I always felt that practicing medicine was my personal, private gift from God. I still do, but I finally understand it's not the only gift He gave me."

She gestured at the open Bible. "Any words you can't pronounce in this week's liturgy? The middle schoolers get a real kick out of you stumbling over Micaiah and Laodicea."

He laughed, setting the Bible aside. "Not this week. It's from Psalms, the verse that ends with 'my cup runneth over.'" He lifted their joined hands and kissed her knuckles, his gaze tangling with hers. "I'd say it's fitting, wouldn't you?"

Freedom. This was what it meant. Worshiping God, loving family, being evenly and happily yoked with Nash.

"Yes," she said. "It fits perfectly."

ABOUT THE AUTHOR

Retired from the post office and married to Duane for…a really long time, *USA Today* bestselling author Liz Flaherty has had a heart-shaped adult life, populated with kids and grands and wonderful friends. She admits she can be boring, but hopes her curiosity about everyone and everything around her keeps her from it. She likes traveling and quilting and reading. And she loves writing.

Find More Books by Liz Flaherty
Website: http://lizflaherty.net/
Amazon Author Page: https://www.amazon.com/Liz-Flaherty/e/B001J919R4
Goodreads: https://www.goodreads.com/author/show/3336348.Liz_Flaherty
Facebook: http://www.facebook.com/lizkflaherty
Twitter: https://twitter.com/LizFlaherty1
Bookbub: https://www.bookbub.com/authors/liz-flaherty
Instagram: https://www.instagram.com/lizkflaherty/
Pinterest: https://www.pinterest.com/lizkf/
Newsletter Sign Up: http://eepurl.com/df7dhP

www.ingramcontent.com/pod-product-compliance
Lightning Source LLC
Chambersburg PA
CBHW051951220626

47052CB00004B/897